FLYING TIME

STORIES & HALF-STORIES

For Chris Brookhouse,
with thanks for
whatever help you
gave Dougald to bring
this out —
Elisavietta Ritchie

Elisavietta Ritchie

SIGNAL BOOKS
Carrboro, North Carolina

Printed in the United States of America.
Revision

Library of Congress Cataloging-in Publication Data

Ritchie, Elisavietta
Flying Time Stories & Half Stories/Elisavietta Ritchie

ISBN: 0-930095-04-9

1.Title.

92-37103
CIP

Also by Elisavietta Ritchie:

THE PROBLEM WITH EDEN

RAKING THE SNOW

MOVING TO LARGER QUARTERS

A SHEATH OF DREAMS AND GAMES

TIGHTENING THE CIRCLE OVER EEL COUNTRY

TIMBOT, a novella in verse

Anthologies edited:

FINDING THE NAME

THE DOLPHIN'S ARC: POEMS ON ENDANGERED CREATURES OF THE SEA

Translations:

THE TWELVE, by Alexsander Blok

GIFT
OF
CHRISTOPHER BROOKHOUSE

ACKNOWLEDGMENTS

The author thanks the publications which accepted all or parts of the pieces in this collection, some originally as poems. All have been revised since prior publication.

"In the Adriatic": as "Legacy" in *Folio.*
"Advice Column": *For Appearance Sake;* as "Portrait of a Woman of Action" in *Pulpsmith, Light Year '86, Poetry Society of Georgia Yearbook.*
"Artifacts": as *"Old Lovers"* in *Modernsense.*
"Benedictus es Domine": *New York Quarterly.*
"Catfishing": *Confrontation, The Unicorn and The Garden,* The Word Works, 1979; *Uncle, Word Of Mouth.*
"Cliff-Hanging": *Raking The Snow,* Washington Writers' Publishing House ©Elisavietta Ritchie, 1982; *Modernsense.*
"Clearing the Path": *When I Am an Old Woman I Shall Wear Purple* Papier Maché Press. *Belles Lettres, The Problem With Eden,* Armstrong College Press, 1985.
"Codicil": *Metropolitain.*
"The Death of the Bishop and Other Transgressions" : as "Economic Measures," in *Word of Mouth,* Crossing Press, *1990. Modernsense, Raking the Snow.*
"The Doe in My Pyracantha": ***Ann Arbor Review.***
"Eel Country": *Tightening the Circle Over Eel Country, Acropolis* Books, © Elisavietta Ritchie, 1974.
"Elegy for the Other Woman": *New York Quarterly, The Unicorn and the Garden, Uncle, What's a Nice Girl Like You Doing In a Relationship Like This, Raking the Snow, Off My Face.*

"Entomological Lessons": as "Staghorns," in *Poetry Society of Georgia Yearbook.*
"Evidence": *Poets For a Livable Planet.*
"Flying Time": a winner in the 1986 PEN Syndicated Fiction Project; *Amelia* (1985 Reed Smith Prize); *Home Planet News.*
"The German Officer Writes a Letter": *Salmon, Passenger, Rage Before Pardon.*
"A Gift from Alexander": *Shore Review, Tightening the Circle Over Eel Country.*
"Gravity Is a State of Mind": © *The Christian Science Monitor* 1992.
"Ito Jakuchu, artist": *Ascent.*
"The Mulberry Tree": as "A World of Purple and Green" © *The Washiington Post, 1980; Tellus; Raking the Snow.*
"Natalie": *Life on the Line: Selections on Words and Healing,* Negative Capability Press, 1992; *The Unforgettable Fire; Yearbook of the Poetry Society of Georgia.*
"Night-Blooming She-Crab": *Modernsense, Tightening the Circle Over Eel Country.*
"October Letter": © *The Christian Science Monitor,* 1989.
"Omens" as "Omens: Southeast Asia " in *Washingtonian, Raking the Snow.*
"On The Farm": as "Dream Sequence" in *Labyris.*
"Overflying Russia": *The American Scholar* © The Phi Beta Kappa Society, 1992.
"Preparing the Feast" : as "A Feast of Eels" in *Dryad, Poetry Society of America Newsletter, Tightening the Circle Over Eel Country.*
"The Puffball Offering": *Denver Quarterly; Modernsense, Tightening the Circle Over Eel Country, Poetry Society of Georgia Yearbook.*
"The Raggle-Taggle Gypsies": *The Poet's Domain.*
"Root Soup, Easter Monday": *Antietam Review.*
"Resurrections": *Poets On: Compromise.*

"In Search Of Eels": as *The Tie That Binds*, Papier Maché Press, 1987 and 1992; *Fundamentals of College Reading: Strategies For Success*, Second Edition, Prentice Hall 1992; as "Walks With My Father", Winner of 1988 PEN Syndicated Fiction competition, in *Village Advocate; The Merchandiser; Love Is Ageless: Living with Alzheimer's Disease,* Serala Press, 1988.

"Sconset Summer": Poetry Society of America annual award 1973; *Ann Arbor Review, Tightening the Circle Over Eel Country.*

"Shopping Expedition": *If I Had My Life To Live Over I Would Pick More Daisies,* Papier Maché Press, 1993; winner, 1983 PEN/NEA Syndicated Fiction Project; *The Miami Herald.*

"Sorting Laundry": © *Poetry* Feb. 1989; *Sound and Sense*, 8th Edition, ed. Perrine and Arp, Harcourt Brace Jovanovich Inc. 1991.

"Sounds": winner, 1990 PEN Syndicated Fiction Project; broadcast over National Public Radio. Excerpts in *Passager, New York Quarterly, If I Had a Hammer: Women's Work,* Papier Maché Press 1990.

"Stable Tales": *Her Wits about Her,* Harper Collins *1987.*

"Swan Story": *Corona, Little Patuxent Review, Raking the Snow.*

"Teatime In Leningrad": Excerpts in *The American Scholar* © The Phi Beta Kappa Society, 1992; © *The Christian Science Monitor* 1992; *The Unforgettable Fire.*

"Tying One On": *Primavera.*

"Urban Services": *Footwork.*

"Why I Wasn't Back in Time": *Redstart.*

"A Wound-Up Cat Always Runs in a Circle Through Snow": *New CollAge.*

"Working The Clay": *Empty Window Review; If I Had a Hammer: Women's Work,* Papier Maché Press, 1990.

"Zurab": *Amelia* (Winner of 1989 long poem competition.)

An earlier version of *Flying Time: Stories and Half-Stories*, was a finalist in the 1990 Iowa Short Fiction competition; "Hunters' Moon" was a finalist in the 1991 Nelson Algren short fiction competition; "Teatime in Leningrad" was a finalist in the 1992 *New Letters* fiction competition, and various pieces were nominated for The Pushcart Prize Anthology.

The author also wishes to express her gratitude for encouragement and help from:

The PEN Syndicated Fiction Project for four awards;

The DC Commission for the Arts and Humanities for four Individual Artist's Grants;

The Virginia Center for the Creative Arts for several fellowships;

And for their editorial assistance: Clyde Henri Farnsworth, Maxine Combs, Mary Edsall, Elizabeth Follin-Jones, Faith Jackson, Ann Knox, Elisabeth Stevens, Dougald McMillan and Ann Schuh.

Grateful acknowledgement is also due Michael Brown of Chapel Hill, North Carolina for book design, cover, and all illustrations.

And to Clyde Farnsworth for the cover photo of the author.

CONTENTS

For :

Lyell Kirk Ritchie
Elspeth Cameron Ritchie
Alexander George Ritchie

FLYING TIME

I

FLYING TIME

"My father is walking today!"

I hold him by his belt as he leans into the metal walker and shuffles one step. I'm startled to be able to see over the top of his head. He used to stand six-foot-two.

"Come on, just one more step."

Watitha Jones, the nurse in the doorway, applauds.

His mind also meanders streets he hasn't seen for years, and he is soon exhausted from the excursion.

Watitha and I guide him into his wheelchair, double-loop canvas straps around the metal armrests, then tie them firmly behind the blue plastic back.

Climber of mountains, swimmer of seas, he always chafed at restraint. Lately, however, he no longer seems to notice the cotton vest oddly dubbed a "posey" after its inventor. Still I hate to see him tied. But some days, with a sudden burst of adrenaline, or as if he could escape the pain, he tries to get up, and might fall again. The hip which splintered when he managed to take off on his own last July still aches.

How one's world shrivels when one is in pain. My back....

"He can only think of himself," the supervisor noted last week. "Existence is limited to his bodily concerns."

And yet...

"The Baron came to call this morning," my father tells me in a low voice. "He brought his whole entourage. We are still in negotiations. We had quite a party. Percy and Gustav and Vladimir and...."

He beams as he relates his friendships with the dead. Several are still lingering over their cognacs and coffee. Then he tires of so much company, and dozes off.

"He had kinda a bad night," the nurse says. "Like he was fighting some war."

"He was a colonel," I explain. "In the American Army, and before that, a recruit in a few other armies. He has indeed fought some wars."

Suddenly a shell explodes and scatters light and alien finger bones. He shouts, screams. The other patients along the hall are terrified, or else unperturbed because they're accustomed, or deaf.

He wakes embarrassed, and confused: he was back at Anzio, Monte Cassino, Normandy, the Battle of the Bulge. Or the Ardennes, Verdun. Though years have passed, his wars fight on. Shrapnel, rubble and peculiar shards of flesh still litter all the bedroom floor so deep he cannot find his slippers in the dark.

"Don't worry, Daddy, that war is over. Everything is all right now."

He looks relieved, but not convinced.

I too despise my patronizing tone.

He indicates discomfort.

"I think he.... "

But Watitha is already half out the door. "I'll come back and change him soon as I finish down the hall. Won't you be staying with him a few minutes?"

I nod, though in fact it is late and I am desperate to leave. Desperate in part because I am agonized to see my father in this sad condition, and the other patients, some worse off than he. Whenever I leave the nursing home, I want to run, jog, bicycle, swim, make love, climb a mountain: whatever is vigorous, exciting, reassuring. Then at home, I have a half-written manuscript waiting, a new job waiting, children waiting, a lover who with luck is also waiting. Multiple worlds waiting like wet canvases. Worlds lively and sane. Worlds that my father shared with me from my childhood. Some, he created.

For the moment, for this long hour, I am grounded by filial duty, and love.

With the nurse gone, in a whisper my father says he is concerned about my alimony. The whispering may be because it is not proper to discuss these personal, distasteful, monetary matters before strangers. Or because, since the nursing home lost his hearing aid in the laundry, he cannot pitch his voice right anymore. Or simply, his voice is weak today. Some days he doesn't talk at all. Reasons vary from hour to hour.

"Yes, I guess I am getting alimony. It will help pay some bills."

We do not discuss the expense of the nursing home which is rapidly eating up what little he saved from a generous life.

"How much cash do you have with you?" He leans forward urgently. "I must pay for the plane tickets. Last night three men waylaid me and beat me up and stole my wallet."

"No, Daddy, that was a bad dream. Your wallet's safe in the drawer. Here."

He struggles to fit the worn cowhide billfold into his back pocket, but it slips between his trousers and the foam-rubber cushion. Of course there is no money in it. The lady down the hall darts into other people's rooms and takes what she thinks is hers, and the man two doors up...

"Your grandsons send their love."

I throw out the marigolds I brought him last week. The water is greeny black, odoriferous, but does not mask the other nursing home smells.

He doesn't pick up on the grandsons. A rare day when I can cajole one into visiting. They cannot bear to come here. Hard for an adolescent to see old people, sick people, other young people incapacitated.

"Grandfather wouldn't recognize us anyway. He is always all spaced out."

Great coughing and hawking from the other bed. The other half of his room is occupied by an eighty-year-old Italian mechanic with, among other ailments, emphysema. Still he smokes on the sly in the bathroom, scattering ashes and cigarette butts and worse across the floor. But he is jolly, usually lucid, and his family never visits. I have brought chocolates for both of them, but since lunch is soon, I stash them in a cookie tin the cockroaches can't pry open.

"We are facing superior numbers," my father whispers, "but with a little more artillery, we can win." His voice resonant now, he redirects the Battle of the Bulge and Tannenberg, confers with Genghis Khan, then again shifts venue and instructs his broker to sell his Edsel fast.

Together we shuttle centuries and shuffle names. This is a good day, I remind myself: he is talking.

"Will you have dinner with me?" The old graciousness. His house was always full of guests. Some he might have met once in Paris or Sarajevo or Beirut. But they would appear, stay a week, or a month.

Where are those friends now?

"I must get home soon, Daddy. I'm working on a science fiction story, this fantasy thing."

He gets agitated, tugs at the straps of the posey, tries to abandon his wheelchair to climb Mount Fuji one more time.

"Too much snow up there at this season," I point out. "Let's wait until summer."

To calm him, I sing, the same old songs he used to sing to me when I was little: Irving Berlin's "Russian Lullaby," "Dark Eyes," "The Old Gray Mare She Ain't What She Used To Be," and anything else I can remember it used to amuse him to sing. Then my voice cracks and I am crying. Fortunately he doesn't notice.

He insists it is time to get dressed to receive the Queen of Belgium, some princess from Cleves.

"But Daddy, you are already elegant." I try not to notice that his trousers need changing. Watitha the nurse promised to return quickly.

"Come on, till guests arrive, let's take a stroll."

I push his wheelchair down the long Lysoled hall to the common room, labelled SOLARIUM although the curtains on the east side are perpetually drawn against a sun too brilliant for aging eyes. The television blares soap operas and commercials for snowwhite laundry, action-packed weekends and eternal beauty.

Parked before the set she cannot see, one ancient lady slips down in her wheelchair until all I can see of her is the untidy knot of white hair with its ridiculous pink bow. Beside her, a grey-stubbled man twisted on a sort of padded cot stares fixedly toward a moribund philodendron. In a yellow plastic chair, an old woman in a pink nightgown rocks a stuffed plush cat and tells it her troubles. A tense grey woman recites a litany of her needs, keeping time by banging the tray of her gerichair.

Near the drinking fountain, propped in an angled high chaise longue and attached to plastic tubing, the twenty-year-old diabetic lies in an irreversible coma from a combination of alcohol and insulin that was not quite fatal enough. My heart tightens whenever I see him. Could be my own son.

I should get on home.

A man shuffles up and salutes. A woman chatters past and winks.

My father seldom seems to notice the other patients. Is the best solution to existence here a retreat into internal exile? Selective eyesight. Dying eyesight.

In the solarium I deal out double solitaire. I can't stand the television and all these people talking to themselves and to the air, so claustrophobic in here.

But the fat-faced clock shows noon. The first food cart is coming off the service elevator. My father's tray is always last, there's time to wheel him back to his room, he definitely needs changing but I can't manage it alone.

Nella, the curly blond medicine nurse flashing gorgeous crimson smiles in all directions, passes by with her cart full of pills and syrups and juices to wash them down. "I'll be over with your medicine in a moment, sweetheart."

With a grand gesture my father kisses her hand, then whispers to me, "Our guests are late! How's our sherry supply?"

The styrofoam cups stick together, but I wrestle four free, set them in a row. The only juice at the nurses' station is prune.

Nella returns with a tiny pleated paper cup of crushed pills mixed with applesauce. "Something delicious for you, honey," she purrs.

I go out to see where the heck Watitha is, she promised...

Out of sight. On her break.

Back in the Solarium Nella is giggling. "He just asked me to fly to Bangkok with him!"

I picture my father's wheelchair grow wide aluminum wings, or his shoulders, skeletal under my hands, sprout feathers — scarlet, orange, green — like a swan sired by a parrot.

"I trust you agreed to fly with him," I answer. "He was once a famous explorer."

She laughs, slaps her broad palms against her white uniform. "Lord, what a crazy i-ma-gin-a-tion your daddy's got!"

"At eighty-five, he has license for madness."

Anxious, his blue eyes watch us. I smooth the wisps of hair on his skull. My mad daddy...

The last food cart is shoved off the elevator. I wheel

his chair to the space at the table between old Mrs. Silverman incessantly screaming "I need sugar! More milk!" or anything for attention, and Muggsy sloshing soup on his neighbor.

I set the brakes, and search for a nurse's aide. "My father's tired, he needs help eating. I must leave. Please..."

Most of the lunchtime shift seem to be on their own lunch hours. A kitchen worker sets down a special tray in front of my father. The nursing home lost his dentures months ago, and the dentist sees no point in new ones, so he can't chew ordinary food.

Although he would rather have smoked eel and vodka, or curry and beer, or beef stroganoff with good burgundy served in a real glass, I spoon the pureed liver, mashed lima beans and fake grape Jello into his mouth quickly before his fingers explore the plate.

"Cheers!" I say, holding the styrofoam cup of prune juice to his lips.

He smiles. "And what about you, my dear?"

"I absolutely must leave, Daddy. I'll come back tomorrow."

The Indian orderly with a diamond in one earlobe promises to change my father as soon as he finishes the trays. Or perhaps he'll find someone else.

To hell with it. My father used to keep a sign on his desk: *Nothing will ever be accomplished if all possible obstacles must first be overcome.*

I wheel him back to his room, somehow hoist him onto his narrow bed, clean him up myself. Something that residents' families aren't supposed to do, a legality about what-if-we-should-drop-him-and-sue. And for modesty, to spare his and our embarrassment. A wife, that should be no problem, but wives don't change patients here. Daughters don't either.

I suddenly recall the only time I saw my father naked. I was four or five, he was late for work and he hurried into the bathroom to shave while I was still in the tub, and he said not to look, then I closed my eyes tight until he left the bathroom.

Now his eyelids are heavy and he is exhausted by the time he is in fresh pajamas.

Then he opens his eyes.

"Thank you. Please inform the general I will return to the front immediately."

And he falls asleep.

Downstairs, on my way out, I detour to the Ladies Room. Inadvertently I find myself in the oversize stall with handrails, high commode and the blue-and-white "Handicapped" sign.

When I too am — "all spaced out" — will there be room enough here for my wings?

IN SEARCH OF EELS

"Hi, Daddy, let's take a walk."

It's a June day in Virginia. My father puts his hands on the arms of his wheelchair, whispers something I can't understand. I try to help him to his feet but he is limp, resistant, heavy.

"Come for a walk, Daddy. *Please.*"

He is shivering. The air conditioning makes the room so cold. I open the window and the breeze billows white curtains into the room. The lawns were mowed this morning and the fragrance of grass wafts inside.

Still he shivers, and murmurs — is it "blizzards?" Then, more audibly, "It's cold, I'm tired. Can't we go home now?"

* * *

Suddenly we're far beyond Lake Shore Drive, in a part of the waterfront I've never seen before. December, Chicago, I'm five, and cold. One mitten's lost. My feet are tired. His legs are longer, he walks too quickly through yellowing snow, gritty slush, toward buildings like airplane hangers with cavernous mouths. Menacing.

He talks about ships, cargoes, distant ports-of-call. Usually I love his stories. He knows everything in the world.

Today I've had enough walking. "I want to go home."

"Just as far as that warehouse." He strides on. "Right foot, left foot! You'll see — we could hike around the whole of Lake Michigan."

"I don't want to hike around *any* of Lake Michigan."

"Come on, hold my hand —Forward, march!"

We reach the warehouse, *shed* he calls it, though it is one hundred times bigger than any shed in anyone's back yard. Crates taller than my father sit on the wharves. By the piers beyond are big boats: tugs and freighters and tankers and tramps. Funnels and cranes, short masts and high booms. Enormous anchors. I keep hoping a sailor will drop one in the water. What a splash. Or else a ship will set sail for the sea.

But these ships are docked with thick hawsers, nooses to choke the pilings. No sails run up those stubby masts. And on Sunday, no one is working.

The nearest freighter bellows and I jump. "From excitement," I insist, "not fear."

This is the most exciting place I've ever been. I could walk here forever. At least until I can slip aboard one of the ships.

Smaller sheds now, smaller boats, a green diner. Odor of smoke, salt, fish. We enter a shack. Barrels of brine, pyramids of clams, crates of fish laid out on ice, eyes terribly wide.

"Daddy, look at that snake!"

"That's an eel. Smoked. We'll take a chunk home for supper."

"*I* certainly won't eat that!"

"All right."

He carries the smelly package. As we walk back, he tells me about migrations of eels to the Sargasso Sea: eels descend Dalmatian rivers, swim across the Mediterranean, then the whole Atlantic, while other eels come from the rivers of North America, until all the eels reach the warm Sargasso Sea. Here they spawn, though I'm not quite sure what that means. My father explains that "spawn" is the proper word for something my grandmothers say people aren't supposed to discuss. But about eels, that's okay.

"Then the baby elvers swim back to the native rivers of their parent eels," he continues, "and renew the cycle."

"Some day I will take one of these big ships. No, I want a real boat with sails. I'll steer it through the Sargasso Sea."

He warns me that in the Sargasso Sea seines of floating algae would entangle the rudder. "You'd never get home again."

Home is already far, Lake Michigan is large, and although he sings old marching songs to encourage me to pick up my steps, toward the end of the journey he lets me ride on his shoulders.

At last back in the apartment, he unwraps the eel, opens his Swiss Army knife (though he could have used the big kitchen knife), and slices hefty chunks.

"I won't eat any," I say firmly.

"Try one bite, just for me."

"I won't like it."

While he hangs up our coats, finally I test one crumb. Awful! Smelly, smoky, salty.

He goes into the kitchen to heat milk for my cocoa, and tea for himself in the samovar from Tula. I test one more sliver. Then another. Then another —

When he returns with the steaming cups, the eel is gone.

Because it is Sunday and I am five, he forgives me.

* * *

Later, I am seven, or twelve, or fifteen. We are walking along the canal, or a river, or best of all, a beach. I mostly keep up. He tells me about everything in the world. We observe frogs, ducks, water snakes, minnows. No eels. We discuss fishing.

At the ocean we cast from a rock or pier or beach. We drop handlines over the gunwales of somebody's boat. Though it is always the wrong bait or wrong tide, on rare occasions we catch a keeper. Then he takes out his Swiss Army knife and teaches me to gut, clean and filet. Our hair sparkles with scattered scales.

We hike along a beach in Cyprus, Alpine streams, a river in Lebanon, the Seine at Bougival. At nineteen, during my college vacation, I fly out to Japan, where my father is working. We climb Mount Fuji. High above the Pacific, and hours up the cindery slope, we nibble seaweed crackers, dried eel, cold rice wrapped in the skin of an eel. We overtake one another, but he reaches the volcano's crater first. I've never known anyone with such energy.

Through years we picnick by various waters and weathers: black bread, odoriferous cheese, a tin of sardines. I eat only my share.

* * *

Time rots like old fish.

Today in the nursing home in Virginia, I beg him, "*Please,* Daddy, just a little walk. You are supposed to exercise."

The nurses are supposed to walk him daily, but are always too busy. I try to walk him whenever I visit, but of late he has seldom felt up to more than a step or two.

"Come, Daddy. Forward, March.!"

He can't get out of his chair. I've forgotten the "posey." I untie the straps, crouch to lift his feet from the pedals, fold the metal pieces that bruise his legs. His skin has become thin and translucent as an onion's.

"Come, now you can stand."

He struggles but does not move. I place his hands

on the rubberized handholds of the metal walker.

"Hold tightly and you can pull yourself up."

He grips the walker. I push and pull, but he still does not make it to his feet.

A nurse comes down the corridor, calling out, "Lunch trays are up! Everyone hurry to the solarium!"

As if anyone here could hurry.

I wheel his chair to the dining room. Some days I sing or tell stories to him, but a "resident" turns the television full blast. He can't hear my repeated "Won't you eat, Daddy?"

He ignores his tray, the plastic plate heaped with tuna and string beans. Everything is now pureed: he has trouble swallowing solids, even the ice cream turning to mush in its styrofoam dish.

I hand him a spoon. It slips from his fingers.

I lift a spoonful of grey fishy stuff to his mouth.

He whispers, politely, "I don't care for any, thank you."

Nor would I.

Time for action. I wheel him to the nurses' station, sign him out for the afternoon. Weeks since he has gone outdoors, the weather is too cold or too rainy or too hot, I have little time between work and travels and children, he has so many "bad days" of late, is often asleep when I've come by. It is a hassle to wrestle him into the car, and with fading eyes and mind, how much scenery can he take in anyway?

Full speed to the elevator, always so slow, out the main door, across the parking lot. An orderly heaves him into my car, and I adjust his seat belt. Though we probably won't stop and get out, he's heavy to handle alone, we fold the wheelchair into the trunk, then, because it is there, the walker.

"Naptime, honey!" The orderly pats my father's shoulder. "He'll sleep like a baby once the car starts rolling along. Just like a baby."

Off we go, down the road, over the bridge to town.

"We're crossing the Potomac now, Daddy. Ahead are the Kennedy Center and Watergate, and to the right — can you see the Washington Monument? Remember when instead of the elevator we climbed the stairs to the top? And here's the Smithsonian — how many rainy Saturdays did we spend in museums? Look at the flower beds — those reds and yellows should be bright enough for you to distinguish. The sky is extraordinarily blue, and the river..."

He doesn't say much to my running travelogue. But I chatter on, while he stares out the car window and occasionally murmurs something I can't understand. I *believe* he is taking in something of a city he used to know well.

We bear southeast from Independence Avenue, pass warehouses, pull in beside a wholesale fish market.

This is surely a futile errand.

"I'll be back in a moment, Daddy. Please wait here for me."

As if he had a choice.

Inside the cool one-story building, men in hip boots slosh around swinging sixteen-pound sea trout and red snappers by the tails. Fish scales fly through moist air. Frozen boxes of octopus and string bags of clams await pick-up by a restaurant. A curly-haired man hoses down the concrete floor. I step over puddles.

They haven't had eels for a year, and before then only rarely and by mistake did any come in with the rest of the catch. Still, I ask him anyway if by chance...

"If you don't mind them *smoked*, Ma'am."

He wraps a large section. I pay and hurry out.. My father may suddenly be panicked by my absence.

Through the car window he is watching with

obvious interest a forklift load crates of mussels into a van.

"I've brought you a surprise."

"Oh, thank you, dear!" His voice is stronger than I've heard it for months. He loves presents, stretches forward for the package. His awkward fingers cannot quite undo the tape on the glazed ivory paper. Still, he clutches it firmly.

"That odor really fills the car!" I exclaim.

"I fear, darling, I have lost my sense of smell."

I drive along the river, find a parking place by the marina, wrest the wheelchair from the trunk, wrestle him into the seat.

"I'd like a bit of a walk," he says clearly.

Stashing the rank package in my purse, I set up the walker in front of him. After much pushing and hauling, gradually he is on his feet. He is unsteady, but gains a sort of balance.

"You made it! That's wonderful. First, take a deep breath. All right? I'll be behind you, you won't fall. Forward..."

He shuffles a couple of steps along the quay. I am steering him with one hand at the small of his back. With the other, I maneuver the wheelchair behind him in case he gets rubber-kneed. He pauses to watch the small sail and motor boats along the river, then manages more steps, a few more. He hasn't walked this far in months. There is a wooden bench ahead, and abandoning the wheelchair, we sit down together.

Again for the first time in months, he begins to talk. He remarks on the red dress of a buxom young woman striding by, he wonders what day it is, he inquires about his grandchildren. Some sort of miracle, this return to "normalcy." However brief.

"And what about your dinner plans?" He invites

me to the Anglers' Inn for supper. Of course I accept: we'll manage somehow. Meanwhile, it is only midafternoon, but he has worked up an appetite.

I run over and buy something like lemonade from a vendor, then unravel the limp smelly paper from the package.

"Look, Daddy. The fishmonger actually had eel today!"

We unwrap it together. I take out his Swiss Army knife, which last year I took over "for safekeeping,," and slice the silvery flesh as thin as I can.

With steady fingers he picks up a slice, swallows without difficulty. Then another, and another, interspersed with swigs of fake lemonade.

"What a beautiful picnic," he beams, and finishes the eel.

OVERFLYING RUSSIA

The green edge of Estonia sickles a line against Baltic waves mottled blue as lapis lazuli. It's July, the water must be almost warm.

There below, in the dusk of winter 1912, my father Yuri, my uncle Ivan, one year apart but close as twins, chopped a hole through the ice. Two little boys in reindeer boots, they cast their lines in.

Ivan sensed a fish on his hook, leaned over, danced with excitement. The ice cracked apart, and he slipped into the current.

Yuri plunged after him, under the roof of ice, thrashed and groped, finally touched his brother, somehow hauled him up, dragged him like a seal to shore.

At this season the dark green forests and fields veined with streams look like malachite.

In the Great War, when St. Petersburg sounded too German and was changed to Petrograd, the boys completed the last class that their military school, the Imperial Corps of Pages, was to graduate before the Revolution. Soon streets became battlegrounds, and every day hundreds were arrested or killed. People began to die of hunger. The Bolsheviks owned the city.

Hiding their noble birth, and knowledge of English, German and French, the boys remained in Petrograd with their sister, mother and grandmother in the apartment across from Tavrichesky Gardens. Rations were shared among ever new waves of relatives, who were welcomed. With every square meter of "living space" already filled, the housing office was satisfied, left them alone.

Their father Leonid, a former general of the

Imperial Armies, whose multicolored medals stretched across his chest, was arrested. In jail he fell ill, and several days later was carried out as a corpse. But the prison guard recognized his former commander, whom he had revered, and secretly carted him home and nursed him back to life. Suddenly deemed of use to the State, Leonid was appointed to the Academy of Sciences in Moscow. Later he was denounced by an envious neighbor and jailed in Lyubyanka.

Meanwhile the boys worked by day loading barges along the Neva. By night Yuri attended technical classes. Ivan filled a stack of old school notebooks with his novel-in-progress.

Ivan also had ties with the Underground and almost got caught but escaped just in time. To leave more food for the rest of the family, the boys joined the newly formed Red Army. They were told they would fight the Germans at the border, but soon realized the Red Army intended instead to fight a civil war.

But the recruiting officer turned out to be a former tutor. He assigned them to guard duty at a beet sugar mill south of Moscow near Tula. They said farewell to Petrograd forever.

The sugar mill was also a distillery and, as they discovered, a covert way-station for White Russian refugees, including various relatives, assigned to petty jobs to appear busy while they waited out the war or waited for a chance to flee south. When the Bolshevik commissar came to inspect, the brothers got him drunk on vodka, and while he slept they borrowed his official seal to forge travel orders for escaping refugees.

The authorities grew suspicious, and the guards detachment quickly moved south to Ukraine, just ahead of an advancing White Army. Meanwhile Yuri and Ivan came down with dysentery. The Red Army retreated, leaving their ill and wounded to welcome the Whites.

Ivan and Yuri enlisted in the White Army's First Drozhdov Rifles Regiment. Yuri was still convalescent, but Ivan rushed to join a company on the ever-fluctuating front lines. He managed to send a letter to his sister in Petrograd: *I know I may die but I will fight bravely. Did you receive my last parcel? Please keep my notebooks safe.*

Yuri followed three days later, but could not locate his brother, who had joined a different company. Soon his own company was fighting against Red Army cavalry charging, swords drawn, through the woods and ravines. Only later did he learn that Ivan's company was fighting at the other end of a pincer movement "splendidly executed and victorious for the Whites though losses were heavy."

Afterwards, while what was left of Yuri's company was resting at a railroad siding awaiting further deployment, a train pulled in from another part of the front. A soldier leaned from a window and Yuri asked if anyone knew Ivan. As the train began to pull away, the soldier shouted, "Ivan was killed near Putivl, the body could not be recovered."

Yuri kept on from battle to battle. His company was not pushed back in any engagement. It almost seemed that their fortunes had changed, and they began marching on Moscow. Then winter brought snow, hunger, illness and cold, shortages of supplies, and more fighting. Casualties grew. When the commander was killed, the soldiers elected Yuri, aged seventeen, to replace him.

Near Kursk, the town of his birth, Yuri was shot through the leg. A peasant rescued him, dragged him by sled to a monastery, then to a railroad junction where the station master's office became the operating room. As the Red Army advanced on them, the wounded were piled onto straw in freight cars and transported ever southward to keep from falling into enemy hands. The Reds were known to torture and kill their captives. By Kharkov, Yuri was dying from typhus.

One fevered night in a field hospital, Ivan appeared by Yuri's cot and announced: "You will survive, and go to a land where English is spoken."

An American military doctor who had volunteered with the White Army, but spoke no Russian, overheard Yuri speaking English in his sleep. Here was a soldier worth saving as quickly as possible. When Yuri awoke, the doctor asked him to serve as his interpreter and aide-de-camp.

The Red Army came ever closer, through the Crimea, pursuing the ragged White Army with its medical unit and trail of refugees to the coast.

Yuri caught the last U.S. Navy ship from Sebastopol. To pay his passage, he had the job of looking after a cabin of Russian orphans an American admiral had rescued and was adopting.

Yuri landed at Ellis Island, borrowed twenty dollars from a sailor to show he was solvent, returned the money and made his way to Washington. He got a job in an auto-body repair shop, then worked his way through college and in time became an American success story.

In later years, recounting his dream, Yuri predicted his brother would reappear just before his own death.

In Paris after the Second World War, Yuri read in an émigré journal a soldier's account entitled "The Death of a Page." Ivan's assignment had been to carry orders from one unit to another. As he dashed across open fields, he delighted in shooting at the Red Army. Then, a fortnight after he had joined the First Drozhdov Rifles Regiment, a sniper's bullet went through his head.

* * *

In Virginia, now eighty-four, Yuri sits tied to a wheelchair, his icicle fingers tugging his afghan. The air conditioner is locked on HIGH and old bones are slow to thaw — but since boyhood he has shivered even in summer. With every day in the nursing home, he grows more confused, words come hard, he barely whispers.

Yet when I came to say good-bye just before my flight, his voice was strong as a soldier's.

"Last night," he reported, "my brother Ivan returned."

Today, as the plane drones on, I wonder: in the haste of war, where did anyone dig Uncle Ivan a grave?

Overflying Russia, I watch field after field unfold below.

TEATIME IN LENINGRAD

One of the earliest games Babushka, my Russian grandmother, played with me on rainy days was Train: we lined up all the dining room chairs, a flowered armchair became the locomotive and a kitchen stool the caboose. The main difference between our Train Game and those in other homes down the street — in St. Louis, in Lansing, then Chicago — was that our train was Travelling To St. Petersburg To Visit Tyotya Mary.

In those childhood days I gave no thought to passports, baggage or the possibility that someone might be following me. Our tickets were small rectangles of colored paper on which I had learned to write *BILLET* instead of *TICKET*, though another playmate who had also learned to read early remarked that the letters looked funny.

I was also the only one of my friends with three names unpronounceable in two very different languages, and two sets of alphabet blocks. Many of the Cyrillic letters looked the same as American letters but some were backwards, had different sounds, or were indeed peculiar.

Even when the Red Arrow pulled into Leningrad, my eternal childhood train to St. Petersburg did not come to rest. An Intourist bus, painted the colors of tomato soup and cream, has brought me to the hotel. A tour is offered for this afternoon, but I've given my excuses of fatigue and my promises to visit the Hermitage another day. I don't like group travel, though it's cheaper, and safer, if tricky to slip off without arousing the curiosity of an omnipotent Intourist guide.

Could use a guide now. In my innermost pocket is

an old envelope addressed to my grandmother, now dead sixteen years, with an almost indecipherable return address. Maps here are misleading, deliberately. I dare not ask too many questions of passersby. Besides, we've had no word from my aunt for several years; useless to attempt to find her.

I walk along the Neva. The sun is warm, gold domes glisten, Soviet women have emerged from their dark winter chrysalises into a gaudy garden of flowered dresses. I scrutinize every passerby, wonder who might be able to give me directions, who might not be too curious about my accent and imperfect grammar. At last I show the envelope, folded so that only the return address is visible, to three boys in jeans. They argue among themselves, the address seems to be on the far edge of town, apparently I have to take a train, but not from this morning's station. They point me upriver, even offer to escort me, but I thank them, I can make it all right now.

Detouring along small parallel streets, I take what may be shortcuts through alleys, past jumbles of broken concrete and across muddy courtyards pocked with old bullet holes. It is far, wherever I'm going. How do these people walk all this way with their bundles, but most of them end up waiting for buses or trolleys. I should take one too but how to determine which number goes where? As for a taxi from the hotel, the driver might report to somebody that one guest who just arrived now for some questionable reason wants to go to the station, and alone, unescorted, take an undetermined train, venture beyond city limits, even to someplace off limits to foreigners.

The River Neva is calm, as if unconcerned how many coups and wars dumped their cargoes of corpses into its waters. From those who died constructing this magnificent city out of a swamp, to those who died in the Nazi Blockade. Rasputin was only one in a long line.

Across the river, the Fortress of Peter and Paul reflects its gold spire on the slateblue ripples. Here, in 1905, my Great Uncle Alexander Konstantinovich was imprisoned, along with a dozen other liberal law students from the nobility, when their links with a revolutionary cobbler were discovered. Their cells were located along "the gentlemen's corridor" and they were not ill-treated. On their release, my great uncle abandoned politics for natural sciences, then became a provincial banker.

This is also where my grandfather, Leonid Konstantinovich, a former general of the Imperial Armies, was imprisoned after the Revolution, a revolution his older brother perhaps helped set in motion.

At moments between boats and ships, when the river is absolutely calm, the image of the Fortress of Peter and Paul is almost perfect, then again falters and ripples. Were I standing on the northern bank of the Neva, I could see the reflections of the Winter Palace stretch across toward the Fortress. As if the mottled reflections from both sides, wavering, never quite touching or superimposed, could hide all their histories. As if by coming here I could discover, recover, mine.

Before World War One and the Revolution, my grandparents knew their way through these palaces. As did their grandparents, great grandparents and all the way back. How often my father, his brother and sister, walked along this embankment, skipping along in their childhood, and later, too quickly leaving their youth, running bent to avoid blizzards of bullets.

My father last saw his sister Maria Leonidovna (whom the family called Mary, in the manner of their English governess) in Petrograd in 1919. Later that year their brother Ivan was killed near Putivl, a village in southern Russia I can't find on the map. In 1920 my father barely escaped on the last ship from Sebastopol, and came to America.

My aunt Mary stayed in their crowded flat in Leningrad with her mother, my Babushka, and her grandmother, my Pra-Babushka, a witty old countess dying of cancer. In the photo that stood on Babushka's bureau, all three generations of women gaze from a circular frame.

My Babushka's face is long and slender. Her mother's and her daughter's rounder faces resemble each other, the same eyes and smile. But a sad smile: from years of extreme hardship, famine, and the special danger to Russians whose origins were an irritant to the new regime. Mary continued her studies in music and history but received no diplomas or formal employment because of that notation on her documents: *nobility*. Like her mother, she lived by teaching and translating.

My grandfather, Dedushka, was appointed to the Academy of Sciences and worked on church affairs in Moscow, until he was denounced and imprisoned a second time. Mary took the overnight train to Moscow, confronted the commandant of Lyubyanka Jail, argued for her father's innocence. He was finally released as an old sick man, and although banished from living in the major cities, he was allowed to teach geography at a university in Nizhniy Novgorod.

From America, my father kept trying to get his family out, buy their way out, but always the Soviets raised more obstacles. And my Dedushka could not, did not *want* to leave: "Russia is my country, in time all this turmoil will pass and matters will be set right again."

After years of war, of prison, of malnutrition, in 1932

Dedushka died of a bad heart. Finally Babushka was offered one of the rare exit visas, permanent, no return. Tormented about leaving behind her daughter who could not obtain a passport, she almost abandoned the idea of emigrating.

"You *must* leave," Mary insisted. "*Now* while you have a chance. In America you will have grandchildren to raise, you must teach them Russian and French. Look, you've been imprisoned twice already, and times will get harder. Don't worry about me, I am young, and strong, and in love with Volodya. We are the new generation, they need us here, we will be all right."

Mary herself had been imprisoned, by accident. Her mother had taken a present of food to some needier friend across Leningrad and didn't return that evening. Given curfews and the dangers of traversing poorly lighted streets, this meant she must have stayed with her friend. But one whole week passed without word. Mary went frantically from the apartment of one family acquaintance after another, whoever she remembered had not fled or been killed, and at last knocked on a door which two militiamen answered.

"Do come in," they insisted. "Your mother *was* indeed here, she just left." Then, without explaining the whereabouts of the previous tenants, they locked Mary into a room for a week under constant surveillance.

Babushka never told me what had happened to either of them, except "They even watched as we went peepee." Accent on the second syllable.

Babushka's other imprisonment was in a jail so overcrowded with nobility that by mistake or design she was put in a cell with prostitutes. She had trouble understanding their slang, but mediated their quarrels, and they liked her so much that when the guards came to move her to the aristocrats' block, the women begged she be allowed to stay with them. Which may have saved her life.

In later years, after her mother's departure, Mary sometimes wrote that she "had to visit the hospital," which meant, in the code she and her mother had established before parting, that Mary was called in for questioning by the KGB. Fortunately, she always "recovered in time."

Otherwise, Mary's occasional postcards — whose black-and-white photos she often hand-painted in color—brought little more than news of Soviet weather, a concert attended, a trip to the Caucasus or Lake Baikal during a break from teaching. She sent Russian children's books to me. She was permitted to receive overseas mail only from her mother, who in turn wrote of my childhood antics and accomplishments, of American weather, a concert attended, and her own travels to the Adirondacks or Lake Champlain, and she could also receive copies of *National Geographic* and successive snapshots of her American granddaughter.

Babushka surrounded herself with what family snapshots she had managed to bring out with her. Dedushka as a young colonel flanked by the two Cossacks with whom he had discovered the sources of the White Nile in 1896. Dedushka as the youngest general, during the Russo-Japanese War. Dedushka reviewing troops with the Tsar in 1911. A photo in an old book showed him in 1914, in charge of some town with an unpronounceable name. Then, circa 1932, on the eve of his last heart attack, an old man in plain civilian suit leaning on a cane.

The early photos of Babushka seemed to me equally distant. I had trouble matching the tall graceful lady in velvet and silk with my gaunt wrinkled grandmother in a cotton frock. In a formal portrait her lap is full of her babies: my round-faced smiling father and his more serious brother still in little-boy curls in their sailor suits, their chubby baby sister Mary in lace and frills. Then Ivan, about seven, his face longer now, and thin, always serious, standing apart from the other children at a family picnic. He looked too young to be anyone's uncle, and I understood he would never appear to fulfill the avuncular role, but I was always to call him Dyadya Iva.

Easier to believe that my tall ever-handsome father was indeed once that smiling boy with soldier-trim hair, beside his brother, both in white cadet uniforms just before World War One. Like their brother Ivan, Tyotya Mary would remain as real and intangible as a character in a novel, forever a solemn girl with dark braids, not "pretty" or "cute" but with an intelligent beauty, standing on the far edge of a world frozen in black and white and shades of grey.

By World War Two, Mary was our only relative in the Soviet Union, and for several years her fate was unknown. Thousands, a million, how many more, uncounted and unidentified, had died in Leningrad during the Nine-Hundred Days of the Nazi Blockade. Only afterwards, from a heavily censored letter to Babushka, did we learn that Mary had survived those terrible times, and received medals for courage.

"Just to survive took courage," Babushka sighed, twisting the strands of white china beads looped around her neck.

During those war years, and the eras before and after when millions also disappeared into prison and labor camps, I remained a well-protected American child in Philadelphia. Still, in 1941 mine was one of the few older fathers in our neighborhood who joined the United States Army, and moreover served in several invasions. So although I was too young to understand properly the depths of my Babushka's grief over the loss of her eldest son and many relatives in Russia's Civil War, and her fear for her two distant children in World War Two, the battle reports in the *Philadelphia Inquirer* were very real to me.

I asked many questions. Some got no answers. Even early I suffered from the intuition, stronger than guilt, that I had missed my destiny, that I should have been born *over there,* to experience what children *over there* should not have experienced. As a Yugoslav journalist later told me, "You should have been born in Europe, you are a natural *partizanka."*

So I lived history vicariously, and only now this warm July morning in 1986, have I managed the enormous step of a flight to the USSR, the first of several trips. First stop: Moscow, then the night train to Leningrad.

All last night the Red Arrow express swayed and clicked noisily through dark forests and farmland. Other passengers in their various compartments slept or tried to, or gave up and read or drank. I hunched on my bunk and stared out the window.

What if I had been born among birches and barricades, gold domes and gulags, in this dangerous land, familiar and strange from childhood, seen the first time in a luminous Arctic July. Would my hedonistic rebellious nature have been tempered by merciless winters, unseasonal famines, eternal threats of prison and war? With whom would I have fallen in love here?

What if my aunt, who loved travel, had appeared on this train, at this hour, could we have known each other? I peered at every old lady in the corridors, in the stations, as on the street now. To mask her noble origins, blend with the masses, would Tyotya Mary have adopted the peasant white kerchief, like a flag of surrender?

While the train jolted on, I looked through a Soviet

book bought in Moscow: World War Two in photographs, black-and-white and many shades of grey. In a 1942 photo of the Siege of Leningrad, women are digging an antitank trench, or a mass grave. One girl lifts a spade heavy with rubble, smiles at the camera. Cheekbones wide, eyes too close, untidy curls. Rib-thin. My double, age ten. A lost cousin? Did she survive the Blockade? Would I have?

The train rocketed on between cabbage fields.

It still rockets now as I walk, as when one has spent several days in a boat, and once back on land, one still feels the motion of the sea and stands with legs farther apart than usual, as if to brace oneself against the slant.

I cross over a bridge and from the center look over the parapet to check if the reflections meet, but a navy or militia launch speeds down the Neva, breaking it into a wake and waves.

At last I reach the Finland Station with its absurd statue of Lenin, arm outstretched as if to hail a cab. There are none.

Many trolley tracks converge, people pour off, people queue to struggle aboard. Hundreds of people mill around the station, they all clutch their string bags and bundles, boxes and buckets.

Which train, which direction? A huge board above the ticket counters lists several hundred possible destinations. I spot the name of the — suburb? village? A ticket to that zone costs thirty kopeks. Fortunately I have the change to insert in a machine which yields a flimsy scrap of paper. But which line, and which track, and which stop?

I timidly ask several young people. No one can tell me, or will. At last an old woman in a brown-and-red flowered dress and white peasant kerchief points me to a track, with a waiting train about to leave. Just in time I jump on the end car.

No compartments, just a car full of wooden seats. They fill up with people and their string bags and bundles, boxes and buckets. No other apparent foreigners.

I don't think I look like one today, dressed in an orange-flowered skirt and a white knit blouse that could have been made in East Germany. Old sandals, bare legs. My only jewelry is Babushka's long necklace of white china beads. I too carry a string bag, with a tan sweater which belonged to Babushka, and a grey raincoat that was my father's. Just before leaving home, I had snatched them from the hall closet in case the weather turned cold.

It's possible foreigners are not allowed to go wherever this train is going. Leningrad is a port city, surely naval installations bristle up and down the coast.

I only hope this is the correct train. I sit on the right side, the better to see the names of stations. Who knows how soon mine will come, if at all. My seat-mates are soon dozing, sheltered behind their *Pravdas.*

The train gathers speed, hurtles along, but in three minutes stops at another station, only a minute, then onward again. Stupidly I'm in the last car so I don't see the station names until we're almost past them. If I miss my stop, I'll never know it. What is the end of the line?

We cut through industrial suburbs, dark buildings without windows or half of them broken, blocks of concrete apartments interspersed with small old houses and construction sites whose workers seem always waiting around for some overdue delivery of materials.

Three minutes later, another station, five minutes later, another, ten minutes, five minutes, another, another, station names fly by quickly, increasingly longer names, increasingly longer times between every stop, now we are out in farmland, broad cabbage fields, people get off, people get on, some seem to be going as far as I am, but I don't know how far that may be, nor where to go when I get — wherever *there* is.

I remember Babushka describing the journey to her family estate southeast of Moscow. They travelled two days by train and when it slowed at a certain road, they would signal, and the train would stop to deposit them in a hamlet. The station master would greet them, the coachman was waiting to load all their trunks and boxes and dogs and even the white parrot in his cage into a troika, or a wagon, or several, and off they drove over snowy dirt roads for a day to get home for a season. During the Revolution and Civil War, local peasants protected the estate. The stone manor house became a workers' club. In World War Two, Nazi officers occupied it, and when they retreated, destroyed it.

Suddenly the right name on a sign, I spring up and jump off as the train is already recommencing its journey wherever.

Not a station, only a siding, in the countryside, somewhere.

Once they had sleighs and carriages here, and farm carts. One cart still, in the weeds. The road between birches and pines is more or less paved, crumbled away at the edges. No sign of a car or a bus, even a bicycle. No people: they must be at work, or hidden indoors. Two or three lovely old peasant houses with airy intricate wooden trim under the eaves, but it's mostly low one-story barracks like shoe boxes tucked off behind tangles of brambles. At some crossroads there are pumps.

A middle-aged woman in grey shapeless dress appears with her bucket. I show her the address.

"I'm looking for an old lady — "

She frowns, perhaps at my use of the word "lady," I meant to say "woman". She points farther down the road, and I keep going. Several times I turn in a lane to look at house numbers, but I'm barely getting warm. Farther on, the numbers painted on the barracks are closer to that on the envelope. Still, there seems to be little logic or pattern to the numbering. You have to live here to know where you're going.

Strangers aren't welcome, strangers are dangerous, foreigners don't come out here. After my sleepless night, I'm tired, and thirsty, and wonder if this chartless — pilgrimage? — won't land me too in jail. I've read too much about the Soviet system of justice, their concern for security.

I try more lanes, paths over hummocks of grass and heaped tree roots protruding from hard-beaten soil. Exploring, I stray from the road, down a winding path. No one around to ask, but I should take a chance and knock at somebody's door. Even as I approach, dogs bark from little fenced yards.

I worry that — even if she has been sent to an old people's home, and I've also read about *them* — my sudden appearance could cause her trouble with the police, KGB. Which is one justification for not having come here in previous years, or tried to contact her ahead.

"But she's old," an ex-Soviet émigré in New York had insisted. "No one will bother her now. Times are changing!"

"Times are changing, yes," warned another ex-Soviet, "but only so much."

Finally an old man feeding a goat escorts me part way down another lane which leads to a yellow barracks with the right number. The tiny garden is a tangle of marigolds, dill and raspberry vines. The barrack-house, long ago painted yellow, stands on concrete blocks. No cellar, must be cold in winter. The tarpaper roofing shows haphazard patches, the steps are uneven stones. At one end of the building, baby clothes hang on the line, broken toys sprawl across the path. No place for an old lady, she obviously moved on and passed on, then younger people moved in.

No point in it, yet the faint sound of — a sonata? — on the television or radio at least means someone's alive behind one of these doors. I take a deep breath, and knock, and knock.

At last a paunchy man in undershirt and shorts unlocks two thick doors.

"Excuse me, but a Maria Leonidovna once lived around here. Could she still be alive?"

"She was yesterday," he smiles. "Can't you hear, she's at the piano again. At least it's not midnight this time. Go around to the other door."

I knock there. A young man with a mass of brown hair answers the door. He is wearing grey pants and striped blue-and-white shirt. He ushers me in without question.

Inside, the small room is dominated by one wall full of books, and another with what must be fifty years of *National Geographic.* A white dog and grey cat sit on the scarred piano bench beside an old woman.

She stops mid-Scriabin, and exclaims in the King's English, "You are here! From America!"

She bursts into tears as she hugs me. I too....

"Let us have tea," she says, though we are so busy talking — in Russian, in English — that we forget refreshments. Besides, the water is turned off during hours when every able-bodied citizen is supposed to be at work.

Her blouse, navy patterned with small white dots, is stained, and held together at the throat with what looks like a cheap brooch. Her navy skirt is patched, but surely she once was as stylish as anyone here. Her legs are heavy, yet she moves like a princess. Her eyes have a milky cast, but what a straight and delicate profile! More beautiful in fact than Babushka, but yes, there is family resemblance. When I was a child, people who'd known Babushka in her youth said I favored her, and I dreaded old age. Do I look now as Babushka did when she left Leningrad? I should ask Tyotya Mary, but with her eyesight...

Tyotya Mary takes a navy beret from a nail by the door, adjusts it over her goose-down hair, as if she needed a hat in order to receive guests properly. No, she never wears kerchiefs.

The table is draped with a paisley shawl. A piece of black bread and a half a cucumber sit on a chipped white plate. A young couple who with their two babies occupy two-thirds of the three-room apartment are nervous with strangers, seldom see foreigners. "Did anyone stop you, check your documents?"

Reassured, they bring out apple pastries. The piano student whose name turns out to be Sasha disappears, then returns with a juice bottle full of his mother's raspberry wine. Other neighbors appear.

"No sugar or coffee in our shops," they complain.

"And the price of black-market sausage!"

"As for vodka — "

"Never mind," Tyotya Mary says, "we will share our rations."

She gropes in a dresser drawer, and under her Bible finds for me a single silver spoon with the family crest. It matches a spoon Babushka smuggled out in her petticoat in 1933.

Without looking, Tyotya Mary cuts the black bread in six exact pieces. Fragrance of...stables? Oats, rye, molasses. Dry, but delicious.

"After all," she goes on, "one must *live*, not merely

reside on this earth. And life will improve after the Nazis and Bolsheviks leave."

"She is old, nearly blind," the young woman whispers as she heaps pastry on my plate.

"She lives in a past best forgotten," the husband adds. "Troubles enough in the present," says Sasha, pouring thimble glasses full of the raspberry wine.

With a steady hand, Tyotya Mary toasts my arrival. She speaks of ancestral portraits I must see at the Hermitage, and how she met Akhmatova in the park, and walked with Pasternak through the woods. She recites Pushkin Byron, Lamartine.

We talk for hours and hours. Outside, the sky remains light as day. The faucet finally runs, and the woman from the next apartment brings an enormous teapot painted with yellow flowers. Someone down the hall appears with a crock of gooseberry jam. Glasses and cups are filled and refilled. Neighbors from other houses come and go, a profusion of food and multi-syllabic names.

Tyotya Mary speaks of her brothers as if they were children still. "Only now that I've lived, can I start to know their lives. They have died, and I learn what it is to live."

During an interval while we are alone in her room, Tyotya Mary searches under her mattress, hands me a bundle of school notebooks wrapped in a scrap of cloth.

"Take these home," she insists, "I can no longer read."

Two-hundred-ninety-six pages. Every page, lined or graphed, is covered with neatly slanted handwriting. But the ink — sepia or purple — is faded, the paper browned, and the alphabet is the old Pre-Stalinist one I never learned.

And what if they search my luggage again at the airport, accuse me of trying to smuggle out dissident manuscripts? And I always intend to fly light.

But this is the novel my Uncle Ivan wrote at age eighteen. I wrap it back in the oilcloth, then in my string bag.

Next she brings out a box of photos she can no longer see, but tells me about each one. On top is a color print of Babushka in her ninety-fourth year, in a navy polka-dot dress and white china beads, in a Florida garden her final Easter. Then black-and-white photos — some duplicates of those Babushka kept on her dresser— of Dedushka, Pra-Babushka, two little boys in sailor suits, a solemn girl, the handsome Volodya who married her and gave her a less conspicuous name. The many mysterious relatives who have not survived. And snapshots tucked among Babushka's letters: odd to see myself as a child, here, as if through a stained window pane. All must have been hidden throughout the years of searches by nosy neighbors and KGB agents, years of street fighting, air raids, displacements.

Sasha returns with his mother. "Your aunt was a brilliant teacher," she says. "Everyone loved her."

Other neighbors reconvene at the table.

"She still helps everyone in the village," says the neighbor bringing a fresh pot of tea.

"A heroine in the Blockade of Leningrad," nods the man from next-door who settles himself in a corner. "See, at her throat is a medal awarded after the Nine-Hundred Days."

They make her show off her other medals adorned with garish bas-reliefs of Lenin and Stalin.

I ask her about the Blockade.

Sasha warns: "Old people exaggerate."

"No," she says. "You children born since the war

cannot imagine the horror. Yet who would believe all we endured? Volodya, my husband, was wounded at the Front the first week of the war. They shipped him to the Urals to mend, but shrapnel splinters stayed in his brain, head pains tormented him the rest of his life.

"For those of us trapped inside the Iron Ring the Nazis flung around Leningrad, bombardments were constant. By night I learned to fire artillery. By day I shovelled rubble into barricades, tore barracks down for fuel, hauled sand bags through the snow. On one slice of fake bread. Some days a thousand died of famine, illness, cold. We tripped on bodies in the street.

"An orphan I adopted perished too..."

"A truce was set to truck the children north across the frozen Ladoga. Still the Nazis opened fire. Before our eyes were children blown apart. I have outlived tears, but not my hate for Germans. Medals cannot hide scars."

She heaps our plates with piroshki.

"Peace returned. And with peace, returned the old denunciations, midnight arrests, labor camps, more deaths."

Sasha interrupts. "I once overheard my mother say that in the Siege *her* mother, dying from hunger, begged the family to eat her. And when she died," he shudders, "they did."

My aunt sips her tea and — the way you might say, *If it's snowing, of course wear your boots* — she shrugs. "Better they ate than buried her. And all winter the earth is stone."

"You must go," a neighbor exclaims. "The last train — "

I rise and because I am suddenly shivering, and she must also be cold, I throw my sweater around Tyotya Mary's shoulders, and the raincoat too. I wind Babushka's beads around her neck. As we embrace, she fills my pocket with chocolates.

With twilight at midnight it doesn't seem late, but the neighbors hurry me out. Sasha will escort me to the railroad siding.

Tyotya Mary remains in the dim doorway, calling out after us, "But where will you hide in the air raid, my dears? And watch your step. Still that awful corpse by the gate."

I grope my way toward the tracks, her candies squashed in my hands, my terrible questions undone.

LEGACIES

I. The German Officer Writes a Letter

My Dear Predecessor:

These three days have proved eventful for both of us. I moved to a new apartment, you had a similar upheaval of relocation.

May I remark that although the curtains look washed and no dust adhered to my gloves; carpets were littered with bits of cloth, buttons, a doll losing stuffing, books foreign and torn, and tatters of scores. Smashed glass cut my heel.

Vital silver was missing but my wife found matching forks at a pawnshop.

She had a time straightening the rooms! At last even the dolls on your daughter's bed are aligned. My little girl is charmed. My son is annoyed to find nothing of interest for him.

In essence, however, the flat is satisfactory, and I compliment you on the Meissen.

It is the violin, though, I wish to discuss. My wife insists that we sell it. Our daughter is tone-deaf and our impatient son has already snapped one string.

But my Great-Uncle Franz played the tuba. As a child after Sunday mass I used to hear his band in the park, and often thought: "How delightful to play some instrument!"

My problem is now: how to procure a teacher. I called the conservatory, what remains of the symphony. A few instructors of course went to the Front. Others simply vanished.

My wife complains that these days I have helped with the move are my first leave in months so how dare I imagine fiddling. And such difficult scores!

Still, someday I will retire.

Should this letter reach you in time, would you be so kind as to recommend someone good.

With all due respect,

II. On the Farm

"The German fleet steamed up river," you told me at dawn. "They had moored in the depths of your dream. They came ashore."

I rubbed my eyes awake.

"A grandmother and a child were sent off to camp," you went on. "They killed your brother and everyone else. Just before I awoke, they raped you."

Day began, your dream dissolved. We drank our tea, and you disappeared to the fields. I planted kale, gathered berries, prepared to can the first tomatoes of summer.

Then the mist on the river lifts. I glance past the bluff and see seven grey hulls, solid and clear.

I'd not known that the greying woman who helped me sort the potatoes was a grandmother till the boy runs up and tells her to pack, they are off somewhere in a truck. Later, I find no one else on the farm.

Suddenly six officers in field uniforms, peaked caps, and dark boots, stomp up the farmhouse stairs. I slip to the kitchen and sharpen the boning knife.

III. In the Adriatic

Years my nightmare persists. The Nazis have come. We've known for months they were approaching.

This time I am running a small Adriatic hotel. Herr Oberleutnant admires my gold-rimmed goblets. I should have cached them beneath the asparagus patch, along with the silver and better champagne.

Meanwhile I try to help the black-haired chambermaid escape through the lines. City hall has become a jail, even the gardener's shack is now a detention cell. Still she wavers, won't leave.

Always that dilemma: to flee — not simple — or go underground, or stay where I am, overseeing my sauces and soups, being polite to the "guests," until the word comes to poison the ferret stew.

This choice is also postponed. Just in time a bulldozer grinds down the street like a tank, and I wake, traces of arsenic dust on my hands.

ZURAB

He stands like a prince in the State-owned vineyard. In the meadows, calves are grazing on chicory and Queen Anne's Lace. Beyond, the peaks of the Caucasus catch the afternoon sun. Is it only the light on rocks, or midsummer snow?

Here in his flat valley, pomegranates, figs, grape and raspberry vines overhang stone walls painted blue. Smoke rises fragrant through wrought iron gates. A red banner hangs from a balcony and proclaims:

ALL POWER TO THE COMMUNIST PARTY OF THE SOVIET UNION.

Young women with long dark hair come out on the balcony, look down and wave, soon descend and surround us like a sea. The women speak only Georgian, but the young man interprets in halting Russian, and we understand one another.

Sudden notes of reed flutes: they form a choir, begin to sing.

The young man says, "Even under Stalin,our cathedral never shut down."

He joins their singing, then slips away down the dirt road to lug baskets of buzzing grapes to the wine press.

A table stretches across the garden under an arbor of grapes.

At dinner he reappears, sits beside me, pours red wine in my glass.

Straight black hair, straight black lashes, black eyes, straight nose, what a smile.

I think: How dazzling you are.

He murmurs his name: "Zurab." Then six syllables ending in "-shvili." Or is it "-adze?" Hard to hear over accordions, drums, a thin-waisted lute he calls a *chonguri*. And roosters with auburn plumes keep crowing even at dusk.

At the head of the table sits the *tamada*, toast-master. The tips of his black moustaches reach almost to his ears. He picks up his glass and toasts the strangers God sends. Then with five kinds of wine, we drink to the harvest, the vintage, the collective farm, to the Caucasus mountains Elbruz and Ararat, to the strangers again.

Women in flowered dresses bring saucers of honey and crusty bread like baseball bats but sagged. Then caviar, smoked fishes, stuffed peppers, grilled lamb decorated with purple basil, three kinds of melons.

"Back in Moscow and Leningrad," I say, "people lack even staples like sugar, coffee and tea."

"Intourist," he whispers. "They provided these fishes and meats in your honor."

We talk of tractors and taxes, quotas for cotton and grapes, and how hailstorms can ruin two-thirds of the crops.

"*This* wine is the best." Zurab pours from a bottle studded with medals. "It won't spoil for one hundred years. Think what it survived! In the tenth century, Persian soldiers surrounded our village. The wine casks were sealed and hidden under layers of clay beneath the cathedral floor. The Persians rode through the portals, camped in the nave, damaged the frescoes, stole whatever gold they could find. But four years ago a workman repairing the floor of the nave unearthed the casks. Archaeologists flocked, tested the wine — this very kind — and pronounced it superb."

"It *is* superb," I echo. "Like melted garnets and honey."

He refills my glass to the top.

He describes his job in the vineyard, the village school, and how slim his chances of attending a technical college off in Tbilisi. "My sister is studying German there, but what's the point. No one like us gets a visa."

The platters are empty, though new bottles appear. The choir down the table sings, then drinkers start telling stories in Georgian. In time they all filter away in the dark.

Zurab recites his verses to me. No matter that I can't understand. He says he would not recite them if I could. Nor if *they* could overhear.

"People get jailed for a poem."

A black cat jumps from a mulberry tree, filches a last scrap of sturgeon from an abandoned plate.

Zurab takes my notebook and sketches his family tree. He relates how in 1941 his grandfather was sent to the Front. Like two-thirds of the men from the region, he never returned. Zurab's grandmother, eighteen then, with a baby, begged the authorities for help in finding her husband.

"He perished," they answered. "Or just disappeared."

No need to add that if the Nazis captured a Soviet soldier and then the Red Army took him back, he was sent to a labor camp in Siberia, or shot.

"But Grandfather might have escaped," Zurab insists. "A few of ours got to America."

"When I get home, I will search," I promise him. "Or at least tell someone the story."

Who knows. In Chicago, New York, or tending his vines in the Napa Valley, an old man might scan an ethnic newspaper in that alphabet like embroidery. He might remember waving good-bye to a black-haired girl in a garden fragrant with jasmine and pomegranates. He might know he left her a daughter.

Zurab says he sometimes daydreams: "Grandfather returns to the village. He carries a shiny suitcase with pills for Grandmother's arthritis, a new coat for

Mama, gold bracelets for my sister, Reeboks and an airplane ticket for me."

Midnight. The cafe has closed. The last waiter watches us with eyes like a lynx.

Zurab turns the page in my notebook and scribbles.

"This is Grandfather's name. And my own. My address."

He walks me toward my hotel, leaves me at the corner. Guards don't let locals in, they report all contacts with foreigners.

"We'll meet by that bridge in the morning. I will show you around the village."

"But my bus leaves in the morning! My plane leaves tomorrow night."

He bicycles home by the moon.

In the morning, outside the bus, he hands me a bottle the color of topaz.

"*Cha-cha*. Our special brandy. My father brewed it from the pulp of the grapes."

I give him a map of the United States, a T-shirt imprinted POETRY above a heron he thinks is a stork, and my fake gold beads for his sister.

The bus revs its motor.

We promise to write to each other.

He disappears before the bus pulls away through the mountains.

Later, at home, I try to decipher his grandfather's name, his own. Something " -adze." Or "-shvili?" Even the name of his village is blurred by a sweet red smudge.

RESURRECTIONS

Far from St. Petersburg now and the brilliant salons of their girlhood, Eugenya and Margaretta, my grandmother's third cousins though we referred to them as The Old Aunts, or The Old Cousins, or simply, Greta and Jenny, sat sipping sweet sherry from jelly glasses and listening to Bach through the static.

Both were skinny and bent as canes, shrivelled as pale golden raisins. Greta wore long braids wound around her head, but Jenny insisted that every two months I cut her hair short as a man's. As nurses, they had looked after hospitals full of people. Now few were left to look after them. While sometimes fussy at over ninety, as the janitor said, they still had all their marbles, and kept their hands busy.

They embroidered tablecloths, knitted sweaters, crocheted covers for kitchen chairs a neighbor had bought from Goodwill and abandoned as tacky. Or they braided ripped stockings — cotton, nylon and silk, beige, black and nurses' white — all together in endless strips which they then sewed into flattened coils to fashion their carpets. Thrift-shop dish towels they stitched into aprons, but as they grew thinner with age, they seamed old aprons into new skirts, which in time split to become dish towels again. They gave me one for each birthday, hemmed in lavender cross-stitch.

The cupboards and shelves were crammed with Since-You-Never-Know-When-You'll-Need-Somethings: empty herring jars and sour cream cartons lined up to hold the mushrooms The Aunts marinated but without salt. Zippers snipped from one dress lay in wait for another. Aluminum foil, washed and ironed, wrinkled in sheafs. Multiple colors of leftover wool spun into a ball. Used shade pulls waited for the day when the venetian blinds would rust through. And dozens of spare corset bones splayed from a dented tin cup: "Visiting children might play pick-up-sticks," Greta said. "And that is the cup that I had in jail."

Nothing was wasted. Last year's Christmas paper rewrapped last year's gifts to them. Lacy bed-jackets never unpacked, lilac colognes and violet soaps too fancy to use, and long cotton panties in peculiar pink, could all be better passed along to somebody younger or more needy *next* Christmas. They did not always recall who had given them which, and I recycled the panties back to them the following year.

They bound the frayed cords of second-hand toasters and lamps with leftover Christmas ribbon, almost setting on fire the Washington flat they refused to let the janitor paint as if for fear of disturbing the dust on the ravelling tapestries. Reassuring the Fire Department it was only a false alarm, I quickly brought rolls of sticky black electrician's tape, and fixed all the wires. And while they were busy frying my gift of a chicken in fat saved from last week's or last year's stewing hen, I shook the tapestries out the window and couldn't breathe for two days thereafter.

Their one silver dish overflowed with long-hoarded Italian chocolates, Hershey's kisses mixed in. Each little square of golden and silver foil was smoothed for some future use yet to be determined.

Meanwhile they instructed each of us what to take when they died. The neighbors would love the African violets, the janitor could use their rugs. The few elegant clothes that their wealthier friends handed down at a season's end were earmarked for me, as was the raw pine desk and bookcase of my girlhood —my parents had given them to The Aunts when I left for college, got married. They could not quite paint over my crayon, ink or first-lipstick marks, nor, surely, discover my secret drawer.

And what shelves of books to distribute among their friends! From *The Decline and Fall of The Roman Empire* to medical dictionaries to poetry, all in several languages, collected over their twenty years in America.

Was this the way their ancestor, the court antiquarian, collected Hellenic statues from Athens, Renaissance paintings from Florence, rococo clocks from Geneva, marble tables from Rome to decorate Catherine's palace? Leftover treasures had graced their parents' estate.

The ancestral home was burned in the Revolution, statues toppled, the rest of the contents stolen, sold or destroyed. They rescued a samovar from the ravaged garden, and had to barter it for one sack of potatoes.

Sometimes as we sat over tea, they related how they nursed the dying on battlefields in two world wars, a revolution and civil war in between, and when the doctor was shot they had to perform amputations themselves, and here are the gold St. George's medals received from the Tsar for bravery under fire, they sewed them into their bodice seams. In the 1920's they had to serve as nurses in Soviet prisons and work on railroads. But this put them in a position to arrange others' escapes and finally their own, in the process smuggling their little niece past the border guards into Estonia and later with Greta to England.

But Jenny spent World War Two trapped in Germany. And oh, how she cherished her dented tin cup in jail! As for one heavy green blanket she had carried through decades as a perpetual refugee —

High time, Greta might interrupt, that they up and died, and one week after a long speech to me on the existence of God in the intensive care unit, she did.

I gave Jenny a new satin quilt the shade of ripe peaches, but she continued to use the old green blanket. The following May, she had me get down from a shelf the pristine quilt, wrap it in white tissue which she studded with silver roses fashioned from candy foil, as her gift for my daughter's wedding. Just two days before that event which, she apologized, she probably could not attend, Jenny finished her sherry, gave my hand a last squeeze, blessed me, and followed her sister.

And The Old Aunts continue recycling. Greta willed her corpse to a medical school, Jenny her ashes into the sea. As executrix, with van and canoe I fulfilled their last wishes.

* * *

This rainy night I must clean out their closets. The building management wants to redo their flat, double the rent at last. "Those dotty old sisters" hung on too long for them. By morning I must haul to the dump the stained carpets, split mattresses, fractured chairs, bags of half-used cleansers and medicines even Goodwill refuses.

Amid wobbly chairs, bits of poinsettia paper and crumpled gold foil, cartons marked for cousins and friends, library books years overdue, dust pussies everywhere, I try on decades of long silk dresses and yellowing petticoats, high-heeled galoshes (their high-buttoned shoes are too tiny), a red velvet cape and huge blue cartwheel hat.

Then in the secret drawer of the desk, I discover a red-and-gold lacquer box. Coiled inside, gleaming and grey, are two long braids I don't know how to recycle.

II

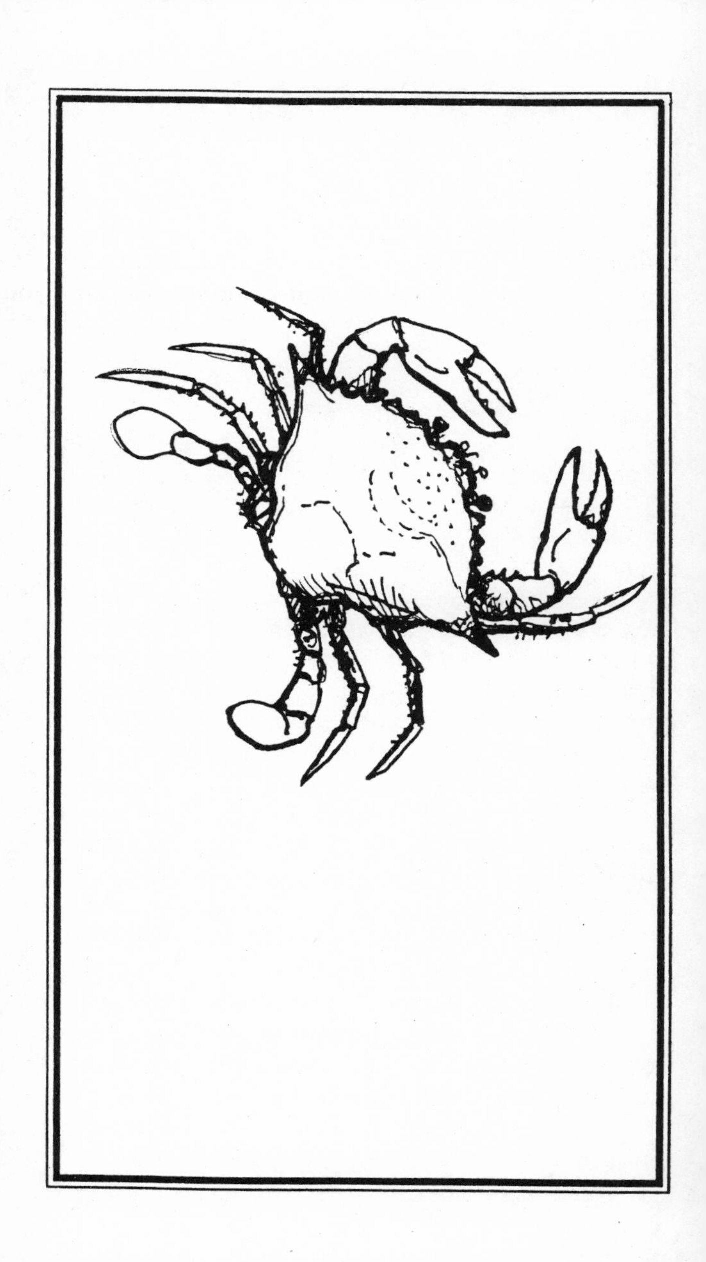

SHOPPING EXPEDITION

"Summer is a dead season," the motel owner says.

What a tropic rampage of life around his pastel pillboxes: scarlet hibiscus and purple bougainvillea entwine with pale clematis, innocent honeysuckle and Virginia creeper mingle with poisonous pink oleander.

My mother's neighbor is waiting outside in his sapphire Lincoln Continental. I watch him from inside, here by the registration desk. He does not seem to notice me. Perhaps he feels it would be indiscreet to be observed leaving a motel with me. He was kind enough to come here for me. He is vain enough to comb his waxy silver hair for me.

My brother took over my mother's Volkswagen when he flew in this morning. He is also not afraid to sleep in her bed tonight. This afternoon he is meeting with her lawyers.

The motel owner is flipping the Yellow Pages for the closest coffin store. This is his first time to have to look up this item. It is also mine.

Finally, among Fruits & Vegetables (Wholesale), and Fuel Ejection Systems, Fund-Raising Counselors, and Furs, we find numerous Funeral Directors. I write down six addresses, thank him, and walk to the car.

My mother's neighbor gets out, shakes my hand solemnly, and opens the other door for me. He squeezes my arm, as if to offer condolences, or something else.

We have talked long on my previous visits. Fortunately now he is saying he does not know what to say. I show him my list of addresses.

"They are scattered all over the suburbs," he points out, "or in the seedier sections of town."

I think of certain foreign cities where one whole street, fragrant with pine shavings and incense, devotes itself to the craft, but funeral revelers gong full blast all across town so everyone knows and in some way shares in the celebration.

She would have shunned such exotic show, as well as funeral parlors.

Cold in the car, I roll down the window, welcome the heat which billows inside, licks the white leather seats with its stream.

"That doesn't help the air conditioning," he murmurs, leaning toward me. He keeps squeezing my hand.

"That doesn't help your driving," I murmur, but he continues to careen through the streets as if late for a wedding.

The first showroom stands among beauty parlors and package stores, used car dealers and billiard halls, in an area my mother would not have frequented. Nor would my mother's neighbor. He is busy unfastening my seat belt with more than condolent warmth.

Outside I am warmer, especially wearing the black silk dress borrowed from my mother, or rather, her closet.

Terribly cold in the showroom. The salesman, dark shiny suit with a faded carnation in the lapel, extols the value of velvet linings.

"But my mother hates velvet, and velvet's too hot for this climate."

"Then rayon, or satin, or best of all silk, see how nicely striped — "

Like Grandmama's love seat, I think.

"Feel here," he says, "how soft this padding is. See how, these handles are hinged for ease of pallbearing."

I think how my brother and my mother's neighbor and her lawyer and maybe her dentist will give a jolly heave-ho, even a *Yo, heave ho.*

"And let's consider oak versus walnut."

Or whatever wood lasts almost forever, and with age might improve.

"My mother insists on cremation: no point in sarcophagi at $4,995.00."

The salesman inhales. "For a dignified burial service—" Distaste on his florid face. He doesn't want his coffins in the fire. He shows me the line in the catalogue that guarantees they are impervious to ground water.

No, as far as he knows, 20 years in the business, there are no reusable coffins.

My brother and I divided the chores: should I have left this one to him?

The salesman steers us from coffin to coffin. Each appears more substantial, more plush than the last. Some have handles of brass.

I remember the padded pink lace Mother's Day card I sent her once, in part as a joke, but also.... It reached her in the midst of her myriad causes. She scribbled back on a pre-stamped post office card: *Why waste your money on such kitsch?* I never sent her another.

In her sensible striped beige dress, she is still lying cold back home. My brother left the air-conditioning on HIGH. That will also keep the flowers from wilting.

She would be annoyed at the stiff bouquets. Sympathy gifts, she often said, should go to worthier purposes. Lilies are so depressing, gladioli too rigid.

On the way home we will surely pass a field or empty lot, I will gather her favorite daisies, as if for a bridal bouquet. I won't let them burn.

"Black is becoming to your fair skin," my mother's neighbor's whispers caress my hair. "But you're pale today beneath your freckles. As soon as we've finished this business, I'll take you to lunch, feed you a juicy steak, or better, beef liver, with a good burgundy. You'll need extra protein and iron to carry you through this ordeal."

How my mother's neighbor sounds like my mother, except that she seldom served meat. It is she who lies terribly pale, back there, beneath her freckles of age.

"They'll fix her up nicely," the salesman is saying, "The pink velvet lining will be most becoming. When the coffin rests open and you approach to kiss her, you'll note the fine workmanship under the lid."

Years since I've kissed my mother. When she was drinking, I couldn't even approach. Despite all her goodness.

I insist that $4,999.00 is too much. So is $3,999.00. Even $2,999.00.

"This coffin is only $2,985.00." The salesman plumps up the plush. "The Basic Package with Options."

The $2,985.00 Package lies at the back of the showroom. Brass handles like door knockers. *Let me in, let me in, in the dead of the night.*

"I know it's a difficult choice," murmurs my mother's neighbor. His fingertips trickle over my forearm. "Shall I help you, honey, make up your mind? And after the funeral is over, and your brother leaves, I could find some excuse to take you for a few days to the beach..."

The salesman is suddenly distracted. His secretary, her coiffure glistening blonde helmet- stiff above her magenta blouse and black patterned slacks, wants him to sign some certificates. He excuses himself, it'll just take a moment in his office.

Another door leads to a smaller showroom crammed with coffins. I explore. Plain pine in the far corner, and what feels like plywood, pasted over with wallpaper, or self-sticking shelf paper, to simulate walnut bordered with teak. A smaller one, gold foil embossed with dancing lilies, sized for a child.

"Prices are much better here!" I tell him. "And it's much warmer away from the air conditioner."

My mother's neighbor is wiping sweat from his neck with a large white handkerchief.

I finger the dacron paddings. Orange blossoms and pink roses, forget-me-nots, and here's one printed with blue anchors. I think of the long-ago pajamas patterned with little green trains, which my mother found at a church bazaar and gave to my brother for Christmas. He never wore them, and before I had grown into them, he passed them on to me unworn.

The salesman hurries in. He looks embarrassed. His long arms try to shepherd us back toward the main salesroom. At the threshold he positions himself, arms folded, between the boxes and us.

"These are coffins for Latinos." His voice is a low surf.

"But my mother was Latin."

He looks with surprise at my blue eyes, death-white skin, telltale red hair. My mother's neighbor also looks astonished. Both are perspiring in the moist air which follows us from the back room.

"She was likewise Oriental and Black."

I point past him. "I'll take — that one over there in the corner, daisies printed on oilcloth. My mother will be happy in that, and yes, I know it is plywood."

Think how well it will burn, I muse, and write him his check. Some question as to whether he will accept it.

Back in the icy Lincoln Continental, my mother's neighbor sits very tall, and does not take my hand.

NIGHT-BLOOMING SHE-CRAB

A flower opening before my eyes, the she-crab sheds her shell so slowly. I captured her at twilight, when the tide was low.

I grabbed her back, then held both claws to bring her to my shack. For she was hard, dangerous. Yet lethargic, splitting at the seams.

The Chesapeake goes dark. I find a match. How slowly she unfolds by candlelight within my plastic pail of sea. Her back swings free now, and she is vulnerable. Gradually her apron opens.

Inside feathered stamens await the pistils of a male, and, eventually, crab caviar. Claws and legs and under side remain encased in their tight carapace. Like a great bud.

* * *

It's late. And I am six, at midnight in Nantucket, eyes blurred but focussed on a rare night-blooming cereus the old sea captain brought home from some South Sea isle. This is the long-awaited night. He and my mother hold their topaz drinks while, struggling not to sleep, I sip at Cokes my mother won't allow at home.

The cereus bud spreads from its sepals.... Ivory petals stretch so imperceptibly, I doubt they move, as promised, right before my eyes.

My mother loves strange flowers. Yet I wonder now: was he so old? All sea captains are, when one is six. And she, was she quite as antique that summer in Nantucket? Why only two of us? Where was my father? What happened when I fell asleep, bathed in the fragrance of the slowly-opening cereus?

At last the she-crab slides out from her shell, glides into my hands. Now slippery as a jellyfish, her innards pulse against my pulse.

The candle shrinks. I light the gas and drop a lump of butter in the pan. She palpitates upon the board. I slice away her head and apron for tomorrow's bait. She quickly cooks, and then I eat my mother, and the cereus.

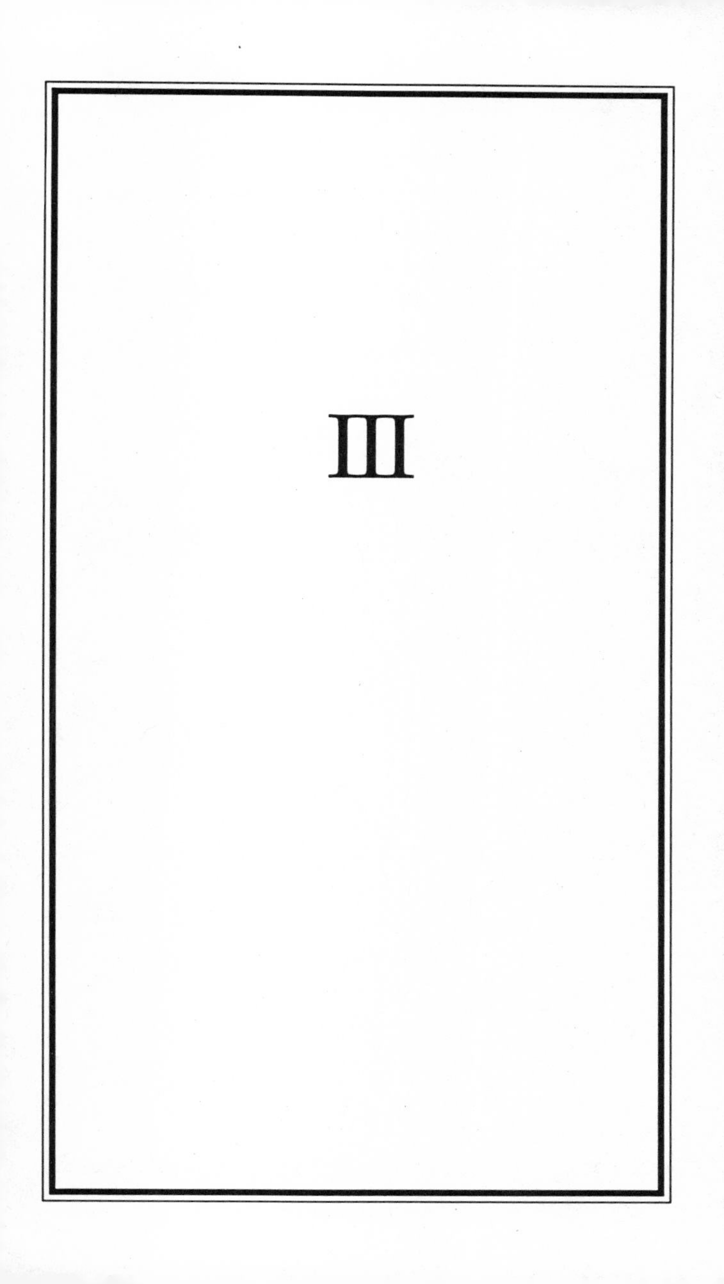

III

THE RAGGLE-TAGGLE GYPSIES

The priests in the Russian church in Chicago were exiles from a revolution old and far. Gold brocade like armor gleamed over black robes to their heels, miters perched like birthday hats on long loose greying hair. Their beards of snowy silk netted blessings, wine drops, crumbs.

Gypsies, exiles also, clustered in one corner, hair tangled, ebony. The men wore shiny colored shirts with unmatched suits, the women dresses blossoming with crimson, fuchsia and magenta roses grown in dreams.

My dress was navy plaid, my eyes were blue, my amber hair hung straight and smelled of lemon soap.

At five, I knew that Gypsies stole small children from the towns they passed. Their vans and wagons, battered, windowless, stood outside the gates. To blend me with the tribe would they dye my hair black?

Eyes of obsidian, eyes of molten tar, watched me edge behind a column, try to move toward safety in the hoops of light from skinny candles stuck in big brass trays.

Priests shook smokescreens from smudged censers, then hid themselves behind a high iconostasis whose saints with sad and slanted eyes stared past my head.

Everybody else closed their eyes as angels chanted high up in the dome.

Candle shadows danced as Gypsies shifted, switched configurations, moved like horses on a plain at night, hummed Romany into my ears.

In that dim church, I disappeared in folds of grimy roses.

Ever since, I've felt the tidal pull between the nomad, tinker, thief, and the stabile shining priests, all of us still far from home.

STABLE TALES

By age five she was already crazy about horses.

They had tried to keep her away from the barns — "Honey, you might git kicked — " but when it was finally her birthday, she was permitted to sit on the gray Percheron. She did not fall off, and since she walked every day two miles from her house merely to hang around, in the course of July she rode every horse in Seven Oaks Stables except the stallion, Big Prince.

"But I don't like to be called Honey," she said.

The stablehands laughed, and hugged her, tugged at her honey braids, and taught her to trot. In her dreams they were cowboys and Cossacks, cavalry colonels, Arabian sheiks.

Were they only old men gone lame from the track, and boys with corn-tassel hair and the warm smell of manure who dreamed themselves jockeys and hot-rod champs?

No matter. Elmer or Joe or Hank would lift her high to the saddle, hold the reins, once more round the ring, and keep a hand on her thigh so she wouldn't, they explained, fall off. She begged them to teach her to canter and jump.

"When you git bigger, Honey," Joe promised. "Not yet."

Warned to stay out of stalls, between rides she climbed the shaky wooden ladder up to the loft where swallows swooped from nests in the eaves. She wasn't afraid of the spiders who tied up the beams. Wasps investigated but left her alone. She tamed the piebald kittens nested between bales of hay, and brought the mother cats Purina Chow so they wouldn't eat up the mice.

When people who hired or owned horses returned from their hour's worth round the ring or out through the fields, perspiring and swatting at flies, she would bring them a chilled bottle of sarsaparilla, cream soda or real root beer from the ice box. Sometimes she got lifted abroad for the horse's final cooling-off walk, or she climbed on the fence to help the stablehands dry and curry their charges.

In the tackroom they let her rub soap on the saddles until the slippery flesh-colored stuff foamed like the cantering stallion. The radio crackled out hillbilly songs, and on a decade of calendars nailed to the walls ladies with silly expressions burst from their glossy dresses. She swore she would never wear lipstick nor grow any breasts.

"I'm going to be a jockey."

"Someday, Honey," Hank argued, "you'll git tired of only a horse between those nice l'il legs."

"Cut that stuff out." And Joe would throw an empty tobacco packet into the cold iron stove.

One rainy morning in August, as usual she walked from her house past the grove of long-needled pines, Tiger Swamp where orange lilies grew, and the willow tree huge as a house, skirted the green soy bean fields and crossed the corrals to the barns. Since nobody hired a horse in the rain, no one was about. The horses ate the damp sugar cubes she extracted from her slicker pocket, then she scrambled up to the loft.

"Here, kitty kitties, I've brought you breakfast!" She climbed the haystack and slid down the other side. "Mother Cat, Mother Cat, where have you hidden your kittens today?"

"In here, Honey!" called Joe, or Elmer or Hank from somewhere below.

She climbed back down the ladder, her pockets bulging with Kibbles for the cats. She ran to the tackroom fragrant with apples, tobacco and saddle-soap, and began to search among dusty horse blankets and saddle pads, as if on an Easter egg hunt.

"Here, kitty, kitties! Where can you be?"

"Here, Honey," whispered Joe, "come kiss this nice pussy cat. Here, down here, in my lap."

She stared, confused, at the strange unfurred thing.

"It's time for me to go home now for lunch."

"Ain't lunchtime yet," he answered. His hands reached for her braids and began to tug. "Jus' come here a minute. And later, if the paddock dries out, I'll teach you to canter. I'll let you ride on Big Prince." His voice became hoarse and he was pulling hard on her braids, "I might even teach you to jump."

"Thank you," she answered politely as she jerked her braids free and backed toward the tackroom door and out into the rain, crossed the muddy corral studded with jumps, then out to the road, past the huge willow tree and Tiger Swamp and the grove of pines, and though it was pouring, and though the car which stopped on the road was only her next-door neighbor, Mrs. Campbell, she turned down the offer of a lift the rest of the long way home.

SCONSET SUMMER

Both so redheaded we had to insist we weren't brother and sister, that seventh summer when we were chased from the deck of our Nantucket ship, splinters from shingles deep in our fingers, thorns catching our freckles when we pitched from the roof into roses that petalled our heads as, nets ready, we stalked the black-and-gold spider.

Then we slid down the bluff to the beach, striking swiped kitchen matches near eel-grass to see: does green burn? All that we asked was one emerald flame.

Yellow and red rippled downwind like tide in a color negative toward tumbledown Squatterstown, dumped under the bluff south of where we lived and swam.

Our crackling orange tidal wave rushed to engulf the bums and the bogeymen, ghosts of sea captains, the woman with twenty-five cats who slept in her stove, the mermaiden's bones we'd uncovered in June...

We commandoed it back to the top of the bluff, buried our give-away heads under vines, heard sirens, peeked out to see three fire engines wind down steep rutted roads. Firemen shovelled sand into dikes just in time.

We were banned from playing together eight terrible days of *Nothing To Do.* Fog thick as smoke kept the bows of our roofs fast aground, but left the charred sand unwashed.

How slowly dunes green again.

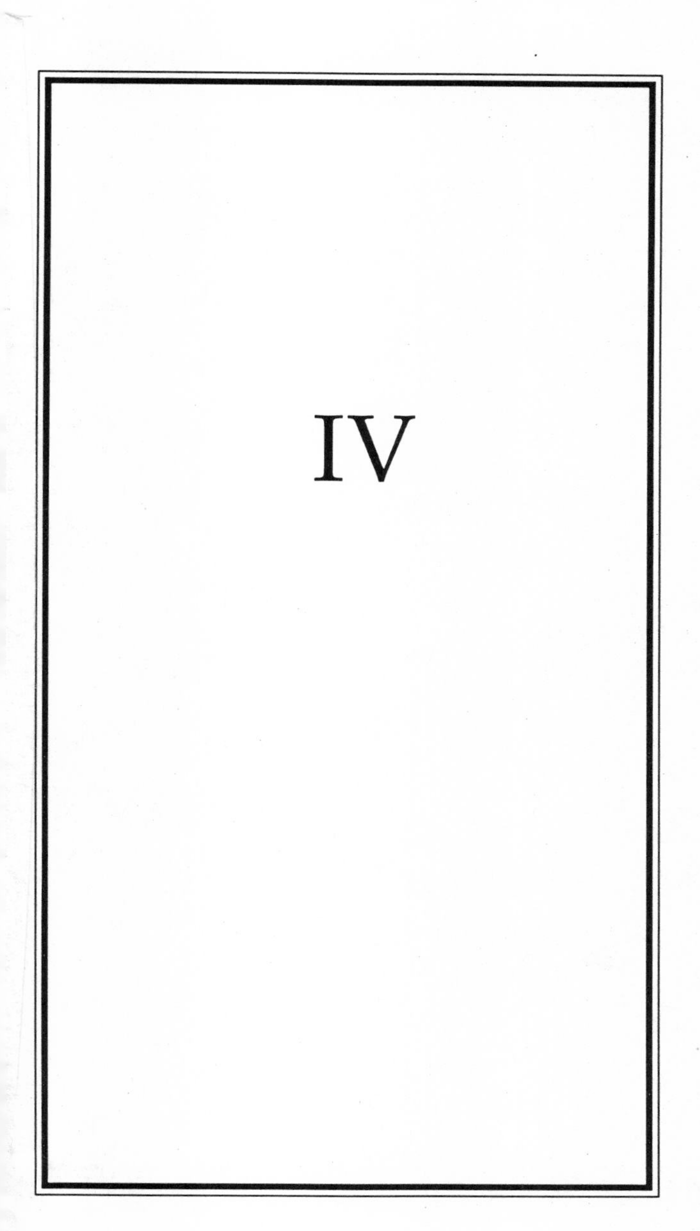

IV

CHILDREN'S HOURS

I. Entomological Lessons

The four-year-old wanted (or I wished for him) a beast more dramatic than one field cricket, Japanese beetle, auburn bristled caterpillar, four pygmy ants, seven clunky grey squash-eating bugs (not the official Striped Squash Beetles).

To keep them in line, we added one black-with-gold-hourglass spider from the fig bush web which held a katydid wound in a shroud of silk. We'd have liked her alive. The spider ignored her new menu, scrambled around our recycled mayonnaise jar, air holes banged through the lid.

I'd read to the child about praying mantids. Now we imagined one stalking across my hand (freckled, wrinkled, tan) to his small, pale, perfect fingers. But mantids come more in September. And I didn't think the sight of those spurred forearms like pliers, mandibles crunching flies, and her mate, was right for a sensitive child.

That August night at the tennis court I captured a staghorn beetle. Huge. Mahogany wings stiff as a snail's operculum. The rhinoceros of insects. Stegosauroid monster of six-legged nightmare. Too ponderous to put up a fight.

What drove or drew him from grass to concrete, the overhead lights? Had the pesticide truck sprayed the lawns?

I slipped him into an empty tennis ball can.

Home in our makeshift terrarium he kept turning turtle, ended up against the round sides of that slippery prison on his back, in which position he died.

Of course we were philosophical, sad. I hate killing anything except mosquitoes and wasps, which I must but prefer someone else deliver the blow. So to be charged with this magnificent creature's death — We'd planned to release our inmates next morning, especially the spider, who caught nothing, no web space in there. We shook out the jar now, even freed the stupid squash-eaters.

At noon the child came with us to the courts. Twelve staghorn beetles lay belly-up, more helpless than horseshoe crabs which they resemble. Under the sun they slowly baked on the green concrete. Three still kicked the air.

We flicked all twelve through the fence to the woods.

II. A Gift from Alexander

A tiny stegosaurus, antennae sensitive, lumbers up your skinny hand. Proboscis crooked, armor gray, crenulated, arched and spiked, elbows/knees right angles, he steps across the recent lawn of fuzz grown on your arm, then stilts across my desk. Six prehensile feet creep up my pencil tip.

"Now," you say, "you've got the writing bug."

I'd chat with you but cycles of unfinished work — larvae, pupae, wet-winged thoughts — buzz and gestate on my desk. So I ignore your hurt look, send you out to play, although I thank you for your fine assassin bug and worry where you've gone.

I try to fence him, but your plated creature stalks across my barricades of papers, rulers, books.

Someday when you're deep in bugs, but I bring gifts and need your love, will you send me away, protected from *my* chatter by a toughened carapace?

III. The Puffball Offering

I found the grass, smashed his ebullience. My world was smashed.

Two weeks we've sparred like damaged gulls clawing in corners, tar on our wings, screeching, or speechless.

One cannot, cannot, live like that.

At last it seems he's put aside alternatives. The weather also puts up a good front before November, so since it's Sunday, we drive to the woods.

Walking alone with his new shepherd pup — childhood snatched back, consolation, bribe — he whistles, throws sticks, spooks the sheep.

Then he discovers a puffball: big as a skull, tanned as the leaves, thumps like a softball. He bears it home as if it were a baby squirrel. Roots like hairs clutch dirt.

My knife slides through that porous sphere. Odd the earth's excrescences should be so white inside. The lead-colored worm doesn't faze us.

Slice after slice we fry in hot butter, eat them only with pepper and salt, hoping, unspoken, for magical journeys but relieved that we stay on the earth, beside our first fire of this fall, and smell mushroom, butter, wood smoke and wet dog.

And we know: this is only a truce, a swift feast of peace, a perching on earth, a brief huddle.

IV. Cliff-Hanging

Today we three scale a hot jungled cliff in Malaysia. An enormous gold Buddha reclines in a cave near the top.

Yet are we still climbing that cliff you slipped from, twenty years past, the other side of the ocean and love? Jealous, aged two, in your tantrum you tore from my hand, away from the rival infant I held in my arms, and, pulling your curls in your rage, you somersaulted under the rickety fence, over the grassy cliff, forty feet down through San Francisco Bay fog.

They shaved your head for the operation. Open-skulled, you lay on the table while they reassembled the chips, worked hours to wire your jigsaw puzzle of skull, pump you flush with my blood. Your pain transferred to my head.

You scrambled back into life, and continue to somersault through a life like the puzzle you smashed. Your hair has grown back, hides our scars.

Today, for some Indian god, we are climbing these two hundred steps green with lichen and moss as those in that colder climate. Heat fogs our eyes now, soaks rampant curls.

You outdistance us. Your sister soon catches up, as she always has, but now jealousy mutes into some sort of love. Or conspiracy?

Far above, you two shrink in the mouth of the cave.

I'm rooted to rock. My heart pounds from these heights. My mind splits with old pain.

Who would lift you out here if you fell? You're heavy for just your sister and me.

Way down at the mountain's base, the saffron-robed monks, who sell orange drinks, trinkets and prayers, are fragile and don't speak our tongue. Any hospital is miles away over bumpy flooded-out roads. My blood is now thin.

You two take so long to explore. Communing with Buddha? Or bats? Or smoking something in there?

I climb the cindery path after you. Like reeling in kites by following strings up the sky. Two gargoyles silhouetted against the clouds!

I will lead you both down, take immense care.

You flip your cigarette butt down toward hazy umbrellas of palms: one mile below? Slowly you turn (you always refused to be rushed, even with birth), pick your way down the cliff.

She follows, then I, in silence. Two hundred slippery steps.

This time we make it all safely down.

V. Natalie

Long before science could sex a fetus, I figured you female and gave you your name. Three months into a sort of life, mere salamander stage, you gave little hint of the brilliant beauty you might become at six, sixteen or thirty.

The doctor warned: "It's not growing right."

So I wasn't surprised, that New Year's Eve, when I bled like a calf under a farmer's knife. All for the best, I'm sure, for us both, lost embryo who would not stick to my persnickety womb. After the doctor's curved blade had scraped your imperfect fragments away, and I awoke, I asked what they'd done with you.

"Don't worry, my dear. But what curious taste...."

I wanted you back to inspect, perhaps preserve in a jar of formaldehyde, like my biology teacher's fetal pig.

"Too late," the shocked doctor replied.

A more appropriate course might have been: a pint-sized plot in the garden beneath the salmon azalea or a lavender hyacinth to fertilize at your own time-release pace. Not plunked in a graveyard with strangers, or dumped in a pit with the hospital waste. Too tiny for priestly blessing. Big enough for my tears.

Each year now seems to bring some new loss to mourn, but I'd mostly forgotten that old one in a distant town. My leftover child, who gave no promises, no expectations, why today do you float in my brain like a salamander reborn in flame?

OMENS

The birds are too parched to sing. The sea beyond the jungle patch is flat.

At least we speak today, although we hold to our opinions in the drought. I watch clouds tarnishing beyond the palms. You claim they'll be blown south.

I haven't watered your hibiscus yet, believing these heaped clouds.

You say the lawn is dust, and I should have turned the hose on anyway: those clouds as usual are frauds.

Beside the well, our neighbor washes her sarong, hangs her colors on the line. She's on your side.

Next-door to the north, the village shaman calls his chicks inside the shed. His bones are old, they know. The praying mantis flexes elbows, waits: mosquitoes come with rain. The air smells wet.

You point out it's been dry three months. The toad stays in the drainage pipe.

A long time since we argued God, or bet on ends of books, or politics.

Birds begin, and soon their songs are drowned by the sound of sudden surf against the beach. Waves rise as if to meet the rain. The clouds invent new animals. They must pause here in their migrations.

And look, palm fronds are flickering!

You say trees always twitch a bit. The heavy cashew boughs are still. The clouds will by-pass us again.

I can't foretell the schedule of the rain, but storms will come. The game of omens won't be settled by a mere typhoon.

IMPASSIONATE CRIMES ECONOMIC MEASURES

I. Elegy for The Other Woman

May her plane explode with just one fatality.

But, should it not, may the other woman spew persistent dysentery from your first night ever after. May she vomit African bees and Argentine wasps. May cobras uncoil from her loins.

May she be eaten not by something dramatic like lions, merely by a particularly homely wart-hog.

I do not wish the other woman to fall down a well for fear of spoiling the water, nor die on the highway because she might obstruct traffic.

Rather: something easy, and cheap, like...clap contracted en route from some other bloke.

Should she nevertheless survive all these critical possibilities, may she quietly die of boredom with you.

II. Urban Services

1:00 a.m. I brake, almost crash.

A possum carcass in the street before the old house of my old husband's new wife.

I'm terribly sad about the possum: smashed up, needle teeth and nose have lost their point, greywhite fur torn, wet, blood like motor oil spread across the asphalt.

I don't like being out on the street at 1:00 a.m., but Police won't cart carcasses away at 1:00 a.m. despite the risk of causing wrecks.

"Just phone the Sanitation Department, Lady, at 8:00 a.m."

So here I am at 1:05 a.m., dead possum, live muggers about, no police protection or rubber gloves.

But I pick up the coil of rubbery tail, guide the nose end inside a plastic shopping bag and tie a knot. A supercan happens to stand in his old mistress' driveway already full of trash so it sticks out beneath the lid. May be next week before a trash truck rumbles up. But so what if it turns a bit inside its grave, I am dancing on mine.

III. The Death of the Bishop and Other Transgressions

You'd be proud how I'm thrifty with liquor now: only one drop stains the brandy glass. When guests look surprised at my penury, I explain: "I killed the bishop."

Or at least, I poured his snifter brimful with your best Armagnac, Drambuie, whatever flask studded with stars. My instincts were generous, innocent; but you were aghast at the waste. When the next year the bishop died, already alcoholic, and far away, still you blamed me for the crime.

Later, when the antique lute you had just given me, (your final anniversary gift as if to play out the forthcoming dance of divorce) fell from the blue-green couch cushion cradling it and broke on the white tiled floor, I was at fault although when it crashed I was three towns away to the north.

That same day you discovered the tiny black kitten I'd rescued from the main road the previous week. Now she lay on our driveway, squashed in the ruts of a car. You accused me of that murder too. Even when our neighbor in tears rang the doorbell to admit it was her Peugeot that hit the kitten, I remained under suspicion.

Now you've gone. Like the brandy, the cat.

I repaired the lute.

Even without you now, I've learned to ration each drop of my life. I barely sprinkle kirsch over the fruit. I keep kittens in, neighbors out, lutes wired to the wall. All is sober, stingy and silent now.

I too avoid any risks. Except those of love. There, I am profligate, and it floods.

IV. The Mulberry Tree

You kept chopping away. First the switches which spring straight up from the branches, then the branches themselves which produced such huge berries.

"All that mess," you complained, "with the berries."

True, we were purple each June, the side of the house purple-blotched, rugs bloodied, clothes inked beyond any bleach from one raid up the forbidden tree.

Guiltless, the mourning doves dined, built skimpy nests overhead. I filled my mouth with sweet fruit, boiled buckets of berries for jam to appease you.

Two new branches grew at the point of each old amputation. Twigs multiplied. Leaves like green mittens in two veined dimensions shaded the house. Moths flocked in the moon. I dreamed of empires of silk.

"Look," you argued, "those branches scratch up my car, that tree is upheaving the house! See, bricks push apart, the sewer strangles with roots."

You sawed through the trunk, left only the stump. All summer the house crouched naked and hot, all winter naked and cold. Then you went away, and the doves. Such intemperate seasons have passed.

But now look. Shoots burst from the stump, branches grow, whole new doubled trunk, and each June more fruit than before.

House and clothes stain purple again. The car is scratched bare. The west wall is pushing apart. The sewer pipe split.

Will I ever wear silk? Will you ever come back? Is it all worth the risk? The mourning doves' nest is as flimsy as mine.

But my kitchen glistens with jars of dark jam, and the world is purple and green.

V. Clearing the Path

You gave up shovelling snow at forty-five because, you claimed, that's when heart attacks begin.

Since it snowed regardless I, mere forty, took the shovel, dug. Now fifty, still it falls on me to clean the walk.

You've gone on to warmer climes and younger loves who will, I guess, keep shovelling for you.

In other seasons here, I sweep plum petals or magnolia cones to clear the way for heartier loves.

Tonight, New Year's Eve, my failing father asks if it's true I am pregnant. I shake my head but he can't see.

One blue-flowered gingham dove dropped from the Christmas tree reminds I'm no more a stuffed duck. Rather a sailor granted liberty in Rio, the only admonition being, "remember galoshes." Otherwise no clock or calendar or globe to warn me where I am or ought to be.

Gold-rimmed and chipped dishes sit in the fetid sink with garlic peels and feta crumbs. The swelling black-and-white cat licks my wrist as if I shared in her complicity.

My boarder's new girl, a zippy brunette, looks me over as I emerge from the cellar. Although I have lived here twenty-three years and carried 23 X 365 loads of laundry up these dim steps, tonight my arms only hold a bottle of elderly wine and two silver goblets.

My boarder is younger than my own son, yet I sense his girlfriend senses a rival. My hair and my teeth are my own and my stockings are black, and lace.

"And who are you?" she demands. "What's your function here in this crazy place?"

I ponder her question, then look her square: "I run this establishment."

VI. Advice Column

When your lover invites you to join him at dinner with his old flame who just blew into town, wear your barest black dress, unwrap black lace stockings, slip on sandals with gold spiked heels.

Choose the jewelry which is unmistakably real, preferably his most recent gift.

Curl your hair, kohl your eyes, knowing you're not as young as you used to be. Hope she is even older.

Stock your purse with expensive perfume, an avant-garde shade of lipstick, and mad money enough to send you all home in separate cabs.

You wonder if you should be the first to arrive at the medium-priced cafe, or give them a chance to talk. Decide this once you will not be late.

Forget you are nursing a fever. Perhaps she will catch it worse.

File your nails to a point, button your long black gloves and sally into the dark.

VII. Tying One On

"You're good at pulling strings," you remark. I'm not sure it is a compliment.

No. I've spent my life, rather, gathering string.

Snippet here, strand there, I'm always picking up bits of string, from trash baskets, hardware stores, post office counters, dubious floors, beaches and ports from San Francisco to Singapore.

Thick hemp hawsers, thin limp string off a pastry box, taffeta ribbons, clothes lines, nylon leader after the fish took off, curtain cords, dental floss, spider strands, scarlet garters, wild grape vines, snapped rubber bands....

"Gathered all that string, all the mismatched bits of life, but," you would point out, "not done much with them."

Yet inch by yard I am connecting all the odd lengths with my repertory of sailor's splices, fisherman's bends, crochet stitches, shepherd's and Gordian knots. And line by line I am winding a huge and multicolored and — yes — a tangled ball.

If you were to unravel it, as sometimes I think you try to do, the string would ring the world, almost but not quite meeting anywhere.

Nor quite keeping anything together. Yet.

NIGHT PEOPLE

I. Visitations

Not as mysterious as 11:11. Still, caught at night when you think numbers would stop their flipping, *4:44* at 4:44 a.m. tilts me off guard. That this phenomenon occurs twice every day, regular as tide, or cows returning for milking, does not alter my astonishment each time — even by daylight — I glimpse those luminous numerals from the side of an eye or square before me, confronted, signalling coincidences. Because of *them,* I am awakened more thoroughly than had it been a mere 4:34 or 4:43.

These hours, the dead return. Less regular than clockwork, they too need their lapses, time off. Before, their corporeal absences provided a time for correspondence as clandestine as our encounters behind the calendulas. Others interfered, raised the risk, tried to cut our connections. Succeeded, sometimes. Not all letters therefore unrolled on paper: many remained imprinted on the gelatinous pages of my brain.

A risk of discovery persists, for, even now, our assignations are garish as calendulas.

Tonight: no interferences, domestic or cosmic. So I will entertain you all. Modestly, singly, during the intervals between 3:33, 4:44 and 5:55 a.m. By 6:66, and the disturbing sun, you must dissolve.

Now, painting my walls magenta, I await your visitations.

You remain in the wings, shadowy, shadowing.

When is our turn to swing from behind the scrim

onto stage? I wait, willing at last to shed my tutu like peony petals.

As if my tangible hands, nicked and nipped, freckled and flecked, could spin you out of the will-o'-the-wisp, shape you like clay, chisel and chip you like stone, re-create you palpable here in my fingers.

When I am old and ache and cannot see, and lie — perhaps in this same bed — half-deaf, half-daft, nonetheless half-dazzled as I weigh my lives, regrets will sift through my fingers like dust. But like a child I will continue to dabble in the mud of remembered passions.

Still unrevealed. Japanese paper buds sealed in the shells of small grey clams. I drop you into a water glass, stir, watch you emerge, swell like sea anemones, flowers in love.

The words for *ghost* and *guest* are similar in several languages. So you return to me in a Babel of voices —

How you roll in, crowding my night! You float about, converse in phrases ephemeral as petals, flutter your hearts like torn kites on twigs beyond that slippery wall. I try to preserve you, in amber, formaldehyde, beg you: *Stay, you told me so little before, or I was too hurried to hear you out* —

And now *you. You* come to me live. But late. No time to stain our clothes unbleachably green from tumbling together in meadows, no time to roll in billowing clouds of quilts, crushing the packed down of swans/geese/chickens under the force of our push and pull, rise and fall, like the beating of their wings.

Time only between these recurrent storms, in the monsoon of a summer of possibilities, for you, peacock spreading iridescent feathers in sunrays through rain, your singular call echoing through gardens of boxwood and marigolds the other side of the chainlink fence.

II. Artifacts

I discover them all over now.

For instance, this noon in a diner in Tennessee, here is one I'd know anywhere.

Chest like a bull, curly brown hair, straight nose, lips sensitive, sensual in a smile, or a pout; skin florid, from sun, or booze; enormous hands, fingers intelligent to more than my own. Though I've never seen them before, even the red shirt, brown vest of leather, worn jeans, are familiar.

But twenty-five years have passed. We have each had successions of spouses and lovers. Still, our annual calls across continents never show up on family telephone bills.

This year was the first I did not reach him on his birthday.

Last year he suffered more heart attacks. He could now be clinically dead.

And the thirtyish man sitting there with a blonde and fried eggs and grits, is probably only his son. So I replace the top on the ketchup, finish my coffee, cold, and pay the tab.

But as I brush past him, still I relearn his particular smell of tobacco and sweat, my humid and stolen days.

III. Why I Wasn't Back in Time

Sweatsuits white, color high, they swing bats and long limbs, jog around the wet school track. Boys, like the boys when I was seventeen, leaping hurdles, eager for experiment.

I drive by as I take my old black-and-white cat spotting blood to the vet. Too many litters: she's wearing out. Cooped in a carrier, she yowls. I know the feeling, forget while I run with the boys around the track, no matter I'm last, I'll make it. And must make it home in time for you, old lover of a decade ago, sixty then, and younger and better than all these pipsqueak sprinters and hitters....

Half a precious hour dribbles past waiting for the vet to finish lunch. I remember my sixth Christmas when, rejecting dolls, I got a microscope, and ask the vet today, "Let me inspect the smear on the slide."

He points out white leukocytes, red corpuscles like doughnuts whose holes are closed, both translucent in the magic light and moving across the pond of glass. No crystals at least. He sneezes, gives me blue pills for the cat.

It's already after I said I'd be home — seldom we meet, always in haste — I race my own marathon back through traffic, the leaky beast purring and growling, slide into home to find on a paper towel: *Where were you? I played your piano an hour then, desolate, left.*

Now you've died, and I wasn't there, and the cat in my lap leaves black and white hairs all over my skirt.

IV. Strawberries

Who comforts the undiscovered lover who mourns in secret beyond the familial circle of grief? I was discreet. Your widow never knew.

Or did that bone sense those of us who are wives seem to acquire with the ring—premonition we'll lose our man an occasional night, at least one unguarded afternoon before Death turns his trick — did it warn *her* of a parallel force?

Men most cherish first loves, they say, also their last. Though you were midway through my spectrum, I fell at your rainbow's end.

But your pot of gold to barter with Death was fast running out.

That May, too late in a life whose limits were set for you (mine promised to stretch forever), over strawberries, first of the year, by mistake we discovered we loved each other.

Then we learned we share the same birthday. We promised the next one together: a strawberry picnic beside warm seas.

You drew sketches, sparked poems. How many more might we have inspired...

No time, with late love, to go stale. By now one's too wise to get caught.

The Peruvian nurse who oversaw your last days (along with your wife, attentive as I could not be), saved me your black briefcase, sketchbook and old red chair when your wife directed them out to the curb with the trash. Granted the case wouldn't lock, the leather was frayed, your drawings were rough, the chair needed recovery.

Had you told the nurse about me? During long

nights when family slept, while she doled your pills and the overripe strawberries left on your doorstep, who could pinpoint which neighbor passed by (no guests allowed in anymore), did you tattle, betray in delirium?

Did you whisper in Spanish, *Deliver these* —Did she just understand? She knew about partings.

Did *she* close your eyes? Or did sleep duplicate itself in the dark?

Each birthday since, as I celebrate mine with friends who, unwitting, fill in, I toast you in silence. Strawberries in my champagne.

A decade now, the red chair still holds your shape, your sketches hold mine in this briefcase covered with moth wings and dust. Summers, heat glues our pages. Winters, mice nibble edges.

Today, early spring, buzzards fly over strawberries ready to pick by our birthdays.

Why did you die just before?

Will I too, here in your chair, sketches and poems overflowing a briefcase I cannot close?

THE DOE IN MY PYRACANTHA

How could she have gotten here? My garden walls are high, glass shards embedded in their crests. Walls divide me from my unknown neighbors, whose homes adhere to mine like endless honeycombs, waxy cells embalming wasps.

The back brick wall separates me from the alley where trucks crank and huff, and dogs perform, and dirty kids throw dirty basketballs which land in my yard and I have to throw them back. Not just basketballs: trash.

Not an alley where one cares to be at night.

Nor did she come in through this narrow house. The double-locked front door is opened only for the rare delivery man. Nobody brought a doe.

Montgomery would know what to do.... Why do you take so long to answer your phone?

"Oh, strangest thing, Monty, this morning when I looked into my garden, there by the pyracantha — "

"The what?"

"Pyracantha. Bush. You know, that evergreen with thorns and tiny white flowers which turn into red-orange berries in winter and the birds eat them, but of course in the city only pigeons and sparrows which don't... The one plant that survives in my garden, and the leaves get sooty. Should hose them off. But they're probably too stiff and prickly for her anyway."

"Did you phone to lecture me on horticulture at 7:45 a.m.? I must finish shaving, eat, catch my bus."

"But what should I do? Montgomery, there is a doe in my pyracantha."

"A...doe? You mean a deer."

"Yes, yes, a real deer."

"How did he get in?"
"She. I don't know."
"You better get rid of it."
"Her. Should I? How?"
"Call the Zoo or something. Now I must get to work."
"Will you ring me back tonight?"
"I'll be...I don't...I'll try. Must run now."
Your phone clicks. Maybe you will call, maybe you won't.

The puddle in my garden gleams platinum in the depression formed when the concrete sagged, and surrounding cement blocks thrust up along their fault lines. Death Valley at flood time. Does it ever flood in Death Valley? Monty would know.

Three sparrows drop to the puddle. The doe's oval ears flick forward: did she also come to drink this isolated rainwater?

So don't dirty things up with your feathers and dust! Whssst! Fly off!

I suppose I must make inquiries. Penalties for stolen property, et cetera. Why are phone directories so confusing? Why isn't "Zoo" in "Z"?

"Information? There's no number for the Zoo."
"Look under Museums, Ma'am."
"Oh.... Thank you."

Museums too turn out to be in an unexpected section of the directory. But indeed, Zoo is there, and after a recorded message providing six alternative buttons even a chimp could push, but all I have is the regular circular dial on my old black phone, at last a human voice speaks.

"Thank you for waiting. How may I help you?"
"I beg your pardon, have you lost any deer?"
"What species of deer?"
"What species are there?"
"Mule deer, roe deer, red deer, black-tailed deer, Indian Swamp deer, Japanese deer, Wapiti, Mazama,

Hippocamelus, Elaphurus, Capreolus, Muntiacus, Hyclaphus, and ordinary white-tailed deer."

"I'm not sure...I just happened to...to notice a doe and wondered if you were missing one."

"Hold the line...."

Yes, I'll hold it until it burns my hands. Through the window I still see you, small doe. You must be thirsty for the puddle, but you won't leave the pyracantha.... Surely Monty will have a solution, he'll tell me tonight when he...If he....

"Is this the party inquiring about the deer?"

"Y-y-yes...."

"Please hold."

Now I wish I'd never.... What if they claim her? Twenty minutes, one-half hour pass....

"Our deer are all accounted for."

"Thank heavens. What should I do now?"

"Whatever you want. It's a free country. Try the Pound."

Click.

Click yourself.

I turn the handle on the glass doors to the garden, slowly, slowly. The doe tenses. My hand freezes. If she takes fright she'll bound away. But where? The walls are too high.

Yet she came in.

Beyond the walls: horns and sirens wind down crowded streets, buses hiss, cars screech, trucks grind. Pneumatic jackhammers drill the street. How did she survive on her way here? Day and night the city is noisy. Always dangerous. She must be terrified.

She must be hungry. What will she eat? The pyracantha is too tough to digest, too thorny for her velvet brown lips.

I arrange, as carefully as canapes: my last leaf of lettuce, eight Cheerios, one Ritz cracker from the box

Monty brought me in June. His last visit here, or was it longer ago? And here is a bright slice of tomato, three blueberries — she'll like them — and the terminal crust of bread.

I inch the door open. She cringes between wall and bush, almost hidden. I leave the plate beside the puddle, retreat. Behind my curtains, surely I am as invisible as she behind her pyracantha leaves. But she knows I am here, I know she is there.

Sunlight filters smog yellow. Pigeons spiral to my offertory plate, start to eat the blueberries, Cheerios. Normally I like pigeons, their varied burnished feathers and babble under the eaves.

I tap the glass, lightly. Must scare the pigeons, not the doe. The pigeons ignore me.

Evil winged things — Shooo!

I go out: only the lettuce and tomato slice remain, pockmarked by their beaks. I refill the plate with the last Cheerios, shove it closer to her bush, settle on the rusted wrought-iron chair — horrid grating on concrete.

Out here in the pallid morning light, I sit motionless, protective. Wait...and wait. Perhaps in time I'll turn invisible....

You almost are, but I can still see your hooves beneath the low branches. I'd meant to espalier them upward against the wall....

Your huge eyes watch me. Even deer have eyelashes. I watch and watch, but you won't come forth to eat. I would reach through the thorns to stroke your head, to offer you biscuits. But you would leap away, scratch yourself on thorns, cut yourself on shards of glass stuck atop the walls.

So I wait, in silence.

A rustle. I move only my eyes, glance toward the top of the wall.

A rat! Size of an otter, or possum. Didn't know they grew so huge.

Must call the Department of Health, or Sanitation, or Extermination.

They would leave their bait, and in the morning, I'd find bloated rat bodies, and dead birds, and what if the doe...?

Shoo, rat! Get away! You won't leave that wall? Then watch this! One pebble of concrete should —

One pebble of concrete flies a good foot past him, but he gets the point, and disappears. Success.

His muzzle pokes up from another niche, then another and another. There are many rats in many niches.

Remember Monty's old cap pistol, somewhere in the attic. Locked for years. Go indoors, quietly, search for the key...Somewhere in my tumbled drawers.... Tomorrow I must sort things out.

The key. It does unlock the stairs. I scramble through the jumble. Ancient ice skates tangle with a sled. Moth-holed blankets wrap mirrors, broken now, be careful. But where is...? Behind these cartons of magazines and photographs and letters from the dead.... Tomorrow I'll throw things out.

The cap pistol is here. The levers work. A half-exploded roll of caps dangles from the hammer. Have they become damp with the years? How long could they keep the rats at bay?

In the garden, the plate is clean. My offering has been accepted. You did come eat while I was inside. You like Cheerios, lettuce, tomato.

But high up on the wall, unhampered by glass shards, the large rat licks his paws.

Aim...Steady...Quickly...Pull the trigger. Pull.

Forgot to cock the hammer. How did the mechanism get so stiff, just sitting in my closet? If only Monty...

Bang the butt against concrete —

An upper window opens in the house next door. "What're you doing with that revolver? Got a permit?"

"Permit? Don't need one for a cap pistol. I simply must scare those rats away."

"I don't see no rats there."

"They must've scuttled off when you opened your window."

"Useless to shoot rats. More always come. Get poison."

"Yes, but my deer...."

"Don't 'my dear' me!"

The window slams.

This is my courtyard, this is my castle. From rent check to rent check.

We must be careful. They might call the Pound, Humane Society, Police.

Stay hidden, little doe, don't come out by daylight. Tonight I'll feed you quickly before the rats come out. I'll keep the rifle inside, unseen, but ready. I'll protect you while you sleep.

You'll need bedding straw. The soil beneath the pyracantha is all cinders and pebbles. You'll need alfalfa to eat. Must look up a pet shop which delivers.

"Alfalfa? Sure. Comes in one-pound and five-pound bags. Sanitized and chlorophylled."

"Oh, my, only five-pound? I'll need many pounds."

"How many hamsters you got? Or did you say gerbils?"

"No, it's a doe and she'll need...."

"A what?"

"A deer." What if I'd said unicorn?

"How did you get it?"

"Her. I don't know."

"You don't know?"

"I'm not sure. I mean, a friend lent it...I'm looking after her for a friend."

"Better check municipal ordinances. Laws against certain animals within city limits. Once was a lady kept a goat.... Can't keep rabbits, or more than five animals without a permit. As for deer, the regulations — "

"The d-d-deer is in the country."

"Then get your alfalfa in the country too."

Click.

Why so rude? I only.... They probably don't deliver anyway.

I'll call the grocery store. I keep so little in the house, I'm out of everything.

"Six boxes of assorted breakfast foods, please."

"Honey-coated or sugar-sparkled?"

"Oh, nothing fancy, nothing sweetened. What do you suggest?"

"We got brands with puzzles and prizes.... Here's one where you can win a trip to Hawaii for two."

How could I take the doe to Hawaii? But they do ship pets.

"Hawaii is fine. Giant-sized. Do you have any day-old bread? And leftover lettuce and carrot greens. Whatever wilted produce you'd be throwing away."

"What's wrong? You're always complaining our stuff isn't fresh enough for you. Just last week you argued the bread was stale. You raising rabbits?"

"Rabbits aren't allowed within city limits. Can you deliver by noon?"

"You think we got a time machine? Noon was two hours ago."

My turn to put down the phone. And I forgot to order tuna or fresh vegetables or bread. I also will eat breakfast cereal.

Through my open door I see you behind your pyracantha boughs. You cringe as the garbage truck clatters the alley, dented cymbals clanking atonally against dented drums. Fire engines howl, police sirens wail. What if you died of fright?

Come inside: You'll be safe here.

You don't deign.... All right, stay there. Nor will I try to approach: Monty has told me that even a deer, cornered, may kick. Someday you will become accustomed to me, someday you may eat from my hand. How long you have survived the city, terrified, but unscathed. Unseen?

I'll go through the attic trunks, find an old horse blanket. Would the smell of mothballs bother you? Behind a splintered umbrella, I discover a pair of doeskin gloves. One blizzard Monty left his gloves with me, went on to warm his hands at other hearths.

This blanket is thick. Here, let me spread it under the bush. I approach so close I can almost touch you—

Skitterish, you edge to the far side. Don't be afraid. Now you can sleep in comfort. Dark will fall soon. Even though the city sky glows peach all night.

Doorbell! Now who?

"Oh, the groceries. Thank you, can you carry them in for me? That's fine, right here."

"What's that you got out there?"

"That? Oh, just a fancy foreign breed of dog. Like an Egyptian tomb dog. Don't worry, they don't bite. Nor bark. I mean: unless a stranger...."

"Thought you were scared of dogs, and your landlord doesn't allow pets."

"I'm only keeping her for a friend, only a little while. It's quite all right."

What if he gossips...or the neighbors...? Even Monty might betray, however inadvertently.... We must be careful.

"Never heard of a dog liked lettuce. Lotsa greens in the bag."

"Thank you. Please—could you shut the door firmly behind you? Good day."

"Good night. See you."

Getting chilly. Sun slanting past the neighbors' dormers.

What will it be this evening, small doe, frayed beet tops or wilted kale? Wheaties or more Cheerios? Take some of both. I will, too. Tomorrow: corn flakes, next day, shredded wheat. We have a lengthy fall and winter to experiment.

Should we move to the country? Must ask Monty's advice. He'll be home, I'll phone now...I'll try again. Again the phone rings and rings and rings. Montgomery is not there. Montgomery, why aren't you there?

There is no Montgomery.

There is only myself. And one doe. In the dusk, soon dark.

I'll leave you my own plate, here, by the door. Eat quickly, undetected. I've got the cap pistol near me to keep the rats away.

Never been so weary....

I'll sleep on the couch, leave the door open, so I can watch you. Perhaps you will be brave enough to come in. Over the threshold. When snow falls, you'll need a shelter.

In spring I'll take you to the country. We'll run through meadows of daisies, the air will whirl with petals and butterflies. All the alfalfa and berries you want.

And in Hawaii, cymbidia and ginger flowers.

GRAVITY IS A STATE OF MIND

"In my other life I am a whale"
Constance Urdang

I am a flyer. No Icarus: a pilot. Not a remote-controlled programmer of those wide-bodied jets where passengers are jammed twelve aflank either, but a hands-on bush pilot at the helm — *stick* — in touch with clouds, the earth, updrafts, and storms.

Watch me fishtail, chandelle, crab the wind, loop the loop and undulate, spiral, pique, porpoise, feather, yaw, hedgehop, roadhop, taxi, mush...

Fat chance. Planes huge and sleek are all that fly me, seldom swerve. All these years my yearning to fly small planes, preferably myself, has gone unheeded. The county airport offers lessons, but I can't justify even their Fly Now Pay Later bargain.

Our neighbor on the Chesapeake occasionally zooms over alone in his two-person plane. His unexpected shadow darkens our tomato, basil and asparagus patch, the roar terrifies the little foxes and every other creature in the fields and woods, then he homes in on the grassy landing strip between corn stalks and soy beans. But although I hint broadly, never has he proffered an invitation to the skies.

So I've soared only second-hand.

In one graduate seminar on Twentieth Century French Literature, the other students snapped up Sartre, Malraux, Mauriac, Beckett and Gide as their mini-thesis subjects. I was about to opt for Camus. But my professor glanced my way and announced, "And *you* will write on Antoine de Saint-Exupéry."

My favorite authors are adventurers, *engagés dans la vie.* Since St.-Ex had lived a life of perpetual motion, barely time out to write *The Little Prince* and ten thicker books, he sounded half-way all right. His biography could certainly be exciting.

"Focus on the *work,*" the professor continued, "not on the author, his influences, social context, historical coincidences. This is a class in stylistics."

She may have tried to explain *stylistics*. The other students seemed to know all about it, and warned me to stock up on index cards. But while I grappled and griped, I didn't grasp it.

Launched into what promised to be a joyless journey, I began to snail my way through St.-Ex's every work and word. Page after page I paused, not just to slice my Swiss Army knife through those uncut French editions, but mid-paragraph to copy on index cards of various pastels, every image, metaphor, simile, repetitive word pattern or phrase. Each category had its color.

That wan rainbow of cards remains stashed under my bed, as if by osmosis I might yet absorb, decode and comprehend their vast veiled message. I haven't. Nor did I complete that course. The only message I received was that, while finally gleaning enough credits for a Master's, I am no scholar.

But St.-Ex was a flyer. From *Night Flight* to *Southern Mail* to *Wind, Sand and Stars* to *Flight to Arras,* his lyrical language, prodigious with images, metaphors, similes and his peculiar turns of phrases, shepherded me though the early decades of flight by stick and compass and stars, even stars obscured by fluffy clouds like sheep, storm clouds like whales.

As his weightless passenger, for months I delivered precious mailbags through blizzards enveloping the Andes, navigated through sandstorms over the Sahara, skimmed seas and trees, and learned both glory and what it is to crash.

I loved St.-Ex. When finally I checked his biographical data, I found we share the same birthday: June 29. I noticed similarities in our writing styles. I still don't comprehend stylistics but I'm grateful for my semester of vicarious flight.

Meanwhile another professor allowed me free rein to study Camus. Somewhere in his *oeuvre* (which I also had to read in its entirety), I found:

If there is a sin against life, it consists perhaps not so much in despairing of life as in hoping for another life and eluding the implacable grandeur of this life.

True, I *have* spent more of my time enjoying "the implacable grandeur of this life" with my feet on the ground, or in the sea.

Suddenly today my feet are in snow. Arctic snow. A last-minute assignment materialized: photograph the historic meeting between two Chukchi Eskimosiy from the farthest eastern tip of what was the USSR, and the Inupiat Eskimos of the farthest western tip of Alaska. My first trip north and I'm so excited I can't sleep.

Now a smallish jet, which flew along the coast of Washington, British Columbia and Alaska, over mountains so dazzling I forgot to photograph them, has left me on a spit of snow-bound sand and grit.

Tucked near the runway is a scarlet plane. Looks tiny enough to hang on a Yule tree or stuff in a Christmas stocking. Delicate. Flimsy. Safer to travel by dog sled, hitched behind a pair of those huskies howling behind the hanger. Or in a more substantial snowmobile: even ten-year-olds are whizzing them over the five-foot-thick ice of the cove.

Cumbersome in my ballooning down snowsuit and elephantine white boots, I'm a spaceperson. Except *I* clump planeward all too conscious of gravity. Can that fragile craft resist its pull?

And what happens to a compass here? My *National Geographic* map of the Arctic shows not only a North Pole but a North Magnetic Pole, and warns in blue print:

Magnetic compasses swing dependably toward this spot and its Antarctic counterpart from distant points but become uselessly sluggish in their vicinity.

Our sluggish course is set somewhere west-northwest from the village of Kotzebue to the hamlet of Kivalina. Fortunately an experienced bush-pilot is at the helm, so far the snow is only on the ground, and gravity is a state of mind.

But at ten a.m., it remains night. Snow hides in black skies. What if a blizzard breaks its traces? Even close, the plane is Lilliputian. Clambering aboard bulked out by all these layers, I feel like a whale hoisting himself into a helicopter.

Inside, the seats are geared for elves. No elbow room to fasten straps. The ceiling must be held together by those random strips of duct tape. The pilot demonstrates how to lock my door, how to reverse the handle and unlock it in case of emergency.

Don't most emergencies happen aloft?

He climbs in the pilot seat, revs the motor, warms it, if not us, up. That propeller is but a giant fan. Wind whistles in through cracks where doors and windows don't fit their frames.

"Not so cold today," he shouts over the engine. "Only ten degrees."

Unsure if he means above or below, Celsius or Fahrenheit, I bless my clumpy suit, clunky boots, three pairs of socks: cotton, wool, and between them, socks made of spun aluminum.

The propeller is spinning, we are in motion, a

bumpy motion on the snowy runway. Like the princess whose authenticity is tested by making her sleep on twenty piled mattresses with a dried pea underneath, I feel every pebble of ice. A bump as we kick gravity aside, rise through ebony air, flying.

Not terribly high. In fact, precariously low over the snowy shore. I feel every current of air, wisp of wind, snowflake.

The sky is no longer so dark, snow reflects waning stars. Here and there, sparkling in vales between conical white hills, are — what? Fallen stars? Beacons planted like flashing buoys to mark a harbor, warn of rocks, guide us...somewhere.

By flashlight I flip open *Terre des Hommes (Wind, Sand and Stars),* which I haven't looked at for fifteen years:

In a plane, when the night is too beautiful, one lets oneself go, one scarcely steers any longer, and little by little the plane tilts to the left. One still believes it to be horizontal when one discovers a village under the right wing. In the desert there is no village. Then a fishing fleet at sea. But in the whole breadth of the Sahara there is no fishing fleet. Then what? Then one smiles at one's error. Gently one corrects the plane's position. And the village resumes its position. One hooks back onto the panoply the constellation which one had let fall. Village? Yes. Village of stars. But...it is only a desert as if frozen, waves of sand without movement. Some well-hung constellations.

Dawn above this white desert reveals, off the port bow, a slategrey, slatehard sea. To starboard lie tundra, snow cones of hills. Careful not to lean too far, unbalance, tilt the plane, I peer down at shadows of polar bears, shapes of whales.

When the sun finally creeps up, it remains behind clouds still programmed to explode their snow.

Suddenly a patch of bare ice alchemized to beaten

gold, shimmers beneath us, almost warm. As if riding updrafts of light emanating from ice, the plane dips and rises, dives and lifts, not of its own volition but the sun's.

I learn to ride the roller coaster of the sky.

Now we are soaring, my head is spinning, and I am in no hurry to return to earth.

Next flight I'll take the helm first-hand.

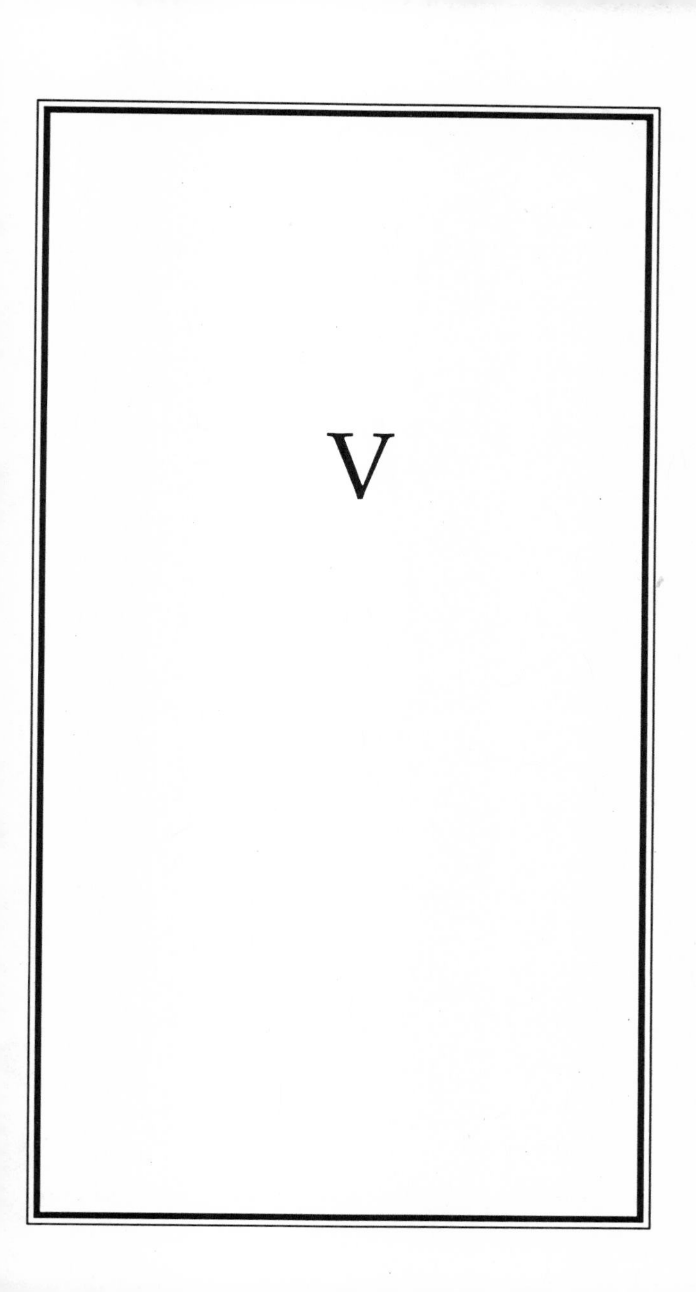

V

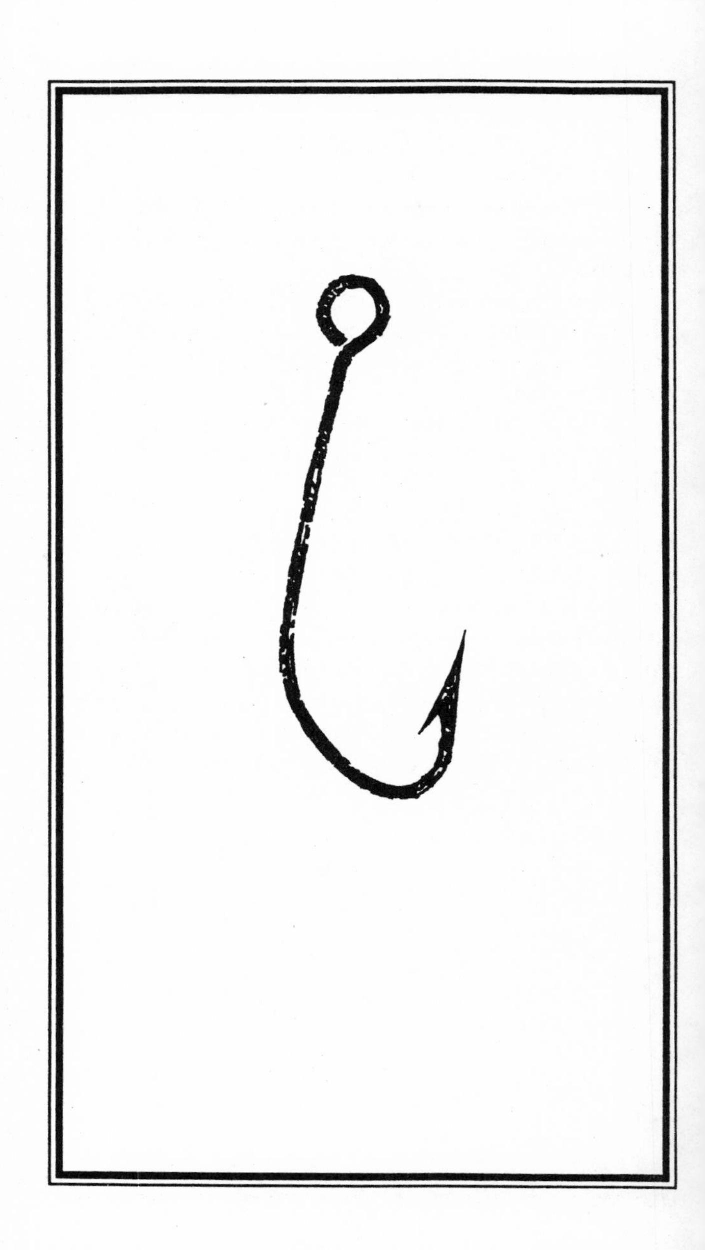

EEL COUNTRY

The beach is coarse with broken shells. Each rush of surf shatters fossils, barnacles and skulls from sandstone matrices.

Husks of crabs cling to strands of algae. Rays glide through shallows, break the waves with shark-fin wings. Ospreys circle, drop, spur fish, soar away to tear them clean.

A driftwood dragon tressed with seaweed lace writhes across a tidal pool, claws outstretched to split the waves.

Beyond the bluff, alive with swallows' nests, a horse with feathers in his mane swims through the waves alone and disappears.

The hidden pond behind the beach is ringed with scrub oaks convolute with vines. Snakes weave through cattails, capture bass. Turtles snap at wading cranes.

Astride her dragon sentinel, a girl with branch and string twists her silver earring to a hook, spears a minnow, flings her line into the cove, and waits.

SOUNDS

Great Aunt Eleanora is giving us trouble these days. She wants to stay on her farm. Alone.

"You can't even get good TV here!" argues the realtor, urging her to listen to a certain developer who will carve the Leighs' Tidewater homestead into twenty-nine lots, whose new owners will presumably install satellite dishes.

Reception is haphazard only because the house is down on the inlet.

Great Aunt Eleanora has no time for television. Radio provides her news and good music. She listens as she paints — currently, murals. She started on murals when she had to stay within earshot of Great Uncle Ramsey, and after thirty years no longer could hide out in the chicken coop, which Ben helped her convert to her studio. There, she painted what she wanted, and the days when Ramsey was in court, shipped the cardboard cylinders of canvases off to a gallery in New York. Ben, and later I, transported the bigger paintings in the farm truck. Her works sold slowly over the years, but we quietly invested the proceeds in a fund which now pays the taxes on the farm. So no need to sell it.

I'm one of the few people who knows this. She assigned me power-of-attorney.

Though now from the rafters a family of black vultures would observe every stroke of her brush, she talks of working in the chicken house again, "once the weather warms and these murals are finished."

Today she shows me the half-painted wall. "Still some baffling blanks, and the moats look empty.

Ramsey suggested lotus and Ben urged lilies, but it's old-ladyish to paint flowers. Last week a stag walked through the snowy yard, then obliged me by standing still — downright posing — under the English walnut while I sketched him onto that panel between the windows. But horses I need to study live again...."

The murals are medieval scenes of knights and their ladies galloping or strolling around various picturesque European hillsides. Frankly, they aren't particularly well-executed, proportions are off, not half as good as her earlier impressionistic paysages, seascapes and passionate abstracts.

But Great Uncle Ramsey Leigh hates abstracts. A retired judge, he likes historic scenes and would wheel his chair, with Ben wheeling along in his wake, into whatever room she was painting. The fact that her eyesight and her hands were no longer as sure didn't matter to them: their own eyesight and coordination were failing. That didn't stop them from advising.

Increasingly Great Aunt Eleanora cared for both men, one black, one white. Ben's grandson Jefferson and I shoved the table against the wall and moved their beds into the dining room, so they would be easier to feed and keep an eye on while she was in the kitchen. With windows on three sides, on bright winter days the dining room heats up, and the fireplace keeps it warm at night. In summer they preferred the veranda, so she continued her murals there.

Then, even with Jeff's help bathing and lifting them, home nursing got too much for Great Aunt Eleanora. Or so the county social worker insisted: "Judge Leigh and that old Ben are two big heavy men, and here you are, a little wren, trying to care for them day and night!"

A private room came available for Great Uncle Ramsey at the Home, and for Ben a bed in the ward.

I thought we'd have a time persuading them to move. But they consulted each other, just as they used to consult over the no-till way to sow soy beans while harvesting winter wheat, and did the barn need a new roof, the mare a new shoe. Finally they agreed to visit the Home: each had cronies living there already, hadn't seen them for ages. They let us sign them in.

"For one week," Uncle Ramsey said. "But just have young Jefferson shove us both into the same room: that'll be cheaper, and we smoke the same brand of tobacco."

The Admissions Secretary blinked, but Aunt Eleanora and I okayed it so the matter was arranged.

Turns out, Uncle Ramsey and Ben rather like being sweet-talked by those pretty nurses, the large-screen color television beats the black-and-white set at the farm, and though old ladies complain, in the Common Room they can smoke without Aunt Eleanora coughing. Still, away from familiar surroundings, they've grown increasingly confused.

At home, though her eyesight is blurring, Aunt Eleanora continues to extend her murals throughout the downstairs. Cats brush against wet paint, leaving her pictures fuzzy and their tails purple and green. I wash the cats and her hair with Tirpolene and baby shampoo, just as she used to wash mine when I was a child. While it was drying in the sun, she would teach me to read from a tiny maroon-covered primer, and how to sculpt and fire the statuettes which remain aligned on an upstairs shelf like ungainly anchors for my soul. While we shelled peas, baked cakes or washed dishes together, she would tell me stories, usually about the great dead artists.

Now I tell some of those stories to a few thousand people, at least in a way, when I write catalogues for the Richmond and other museums. And she tells them aloud to herself as she cooks what she needs to feed herself and twenty-six (at last count) cats.

Jefferson, who bought the old tenant house, cuts fallen branches into logs small enough for her to put in the old stove. He also ploughs her road after snows, when he is around, and some Wednesdays his wife Alethea Mae brings groceries. I come by most weekends with a cake or casserole to last several days. Since her washing machine rusted through, I do her laundry in town. I lug my computer to manage her bills and the correspondence which still comes in from galleries and other artists. I also bring new brushes and paints, and sometimes, friends for a picnic. She prefers young people. And anyone who wants to take home a kitten or two, Great Aunt Eleanora will offer them their choice.

At her request, every visit I check on the farm, attempt to patch whatever needs patching. During my childhood summers here, Ben used to let Jeff and me tag along to "help", soon taught us to work with wrench and saw, tractor and scythe. So last week Jeff and I shored up the sun porch, but another board's always rotten somewhere. The roof leaks into the upstairs bedrooms, though since she's had trouble with steps, Great Aunt Eleanora now sleeps off the kitchen, where Ben lived until his legs gave out. In winter the furnace tends to die, or the chimney gets blocked as when thirteen bricks fell into the flue, and the sweep also removed thirteen buckets of soot. The electricity fails in storms, the circulating pump breaks, the septic tank —

More than one midnight I've driven from Richmond at 65 m.p.h. to cope. And some night, it will be that Aunt Eleanora has tripped over a cat and broken a hip, or wandered to the beach and waded in too far.

So of course I'm concerned about her, out here all alone now, fields on three sides, the inlet on the fourth.

"Just sell the place," people urge, "move her into the Home, and you won't have any more worries."

Since I am her closest relative, everyone is pressuring me. Sometimes I'm tempted. A terrible decision, to wrest her from her beloved farm.

Today I bring up the move.

"I am perfectly fine here, thank you."

January's wind methodically flaps the shed roof, beats crepe myrtle branches against the house, rattles windows — three panes slipped from their sashes as the putty crumbled, and the glazier is always coming next week. Cats meowl to enter or exit, I suspect some other animal in the cellar, the forgotten tea kettle shrills, even the chicken soup I'm cooking makes unearthly burbles.

"But don't all the odd noises bother you at night?"

"At night," she shrugs, "of course there are sounds. Mostly, I identify: from the woods, the hoot owl. From the cove, loons. Scratchings, shrills, chirps in the roof, wind spiralling down all three chimneys — each has a singular moan. And when I pry rot from a window frame, the squeal that freezes against the pane is explainable."

Since Aunt Eleanora is much alone, whenever she has company, she really talks.

"But — " she pauses to pour hot water into the pot, not noticing it splash on the worn Oriental rug, "it's the voices the farm has absorbed across three hundred years — just imagine, from Indian plaints to colonial cries of love! Then this morning when I looked out the kitchen door to see if you had arrived, I noticed among the spindly figs and runaway vines covering the foundations of that first plantation house here (you remember the one that burned in the Civil War, and nowhere in the archives could Ramsey ever discover which side lighted the torch) — I noticed a child in a dark pink pinafore."

"What child?" The nearest house is a mile away, no children there. No picnickers land on her beach in January.

"A child...plump, about three. She was crying, her nose was running, she had a cold, or was cold. Then, she was gone.... Or, was never there."

"Perhaps not...."

"But every spring when the garden is ploughed, in a furrow near — remember that broken pipe which leads to the barn? — always I find one tattered rag doll. You might check in the pony cart."

Except for Ramsey's ancient Packard and the farmer's tractor, the barn has stood empty for years. But the wood is good, and the stalls still bear the names of horses I learned to ride on: SMOKEY, STORM KING, OLD JESS.

Could raise horses again, someday....

Absently cradling an orange kitten named Titian, Aunt Eleanora stares toward the river. Can she see two black vultures in the moribund oak?

I pour tea into chipped china cups. "But aren't you ever afraid here?"

"Afraid? Of — ghosts? Nonsense. I early learned to settle in with presences. As with the woodchucks in the cellar, raccoons in the roof, cats in the barn their ancestors guard. In time," she sighs, "my voices too will merge with the farm."

"Voices? Did you discuss this with the doctor?"

She looks puzzled. "The — voices? Whatever for? And it's not always voices. Mostly, it's like your computer pinging even if the power's off, or high-tension lines humming across the fields in a blizzard."

"Ringing in the ears can mean something's wrong."

"I meant to mention it to the doctor last year. Happens whenever I close my eyes. A hive in the brain." Her blue eyes focus on me. "You must hear them too. As in town, there's always an ambulance down the avenue, fire engines across the park, jack-hammers, traffic, that school yard six blocks away, hooves striking cobblestones."

"Except the cobblestones were asphalted over years ago, and there aren't horses in town anymore."

"Sounds pile up, you know, are stored. Volcanoes exploding decades ago remain in the air. Cathedral chimes, troubadours' plaints, street cries. High-pitched notes that set dogs howling. That's what I hear, when I wake in the night or try to nap after lunch. A music box under my pillow, roosters behind the drapes. I wonder, has my skull become one vast receptor...."

Suddenly she looks concerned. "Do I also transmit?"

"Transmit?" The social worker may well be correct: incipient senility.

"I certainly don't generate. I nap in the armchair — no creaky rocker for me — radio off, phone off the hook. My necklaces which used to tinkle and jangle — I moved like a belled goat — have been stolen. Or sold?"

"You gave them all to me, Aunt Eleanora, don't you remember, one every birthday for the last twenty years. But I'll return them, you obviously miss them, I don't need more than one."

Once she goes into the Home, any jewelry will disappear.

"Oh, don't worry about returning those baubles, dear. I can still hear their symphonies on my bare neck. Lovely.... Yes, the doctor suggested tests my next check-up, next year. Today," — she looks radiant — "Today, I'm tuned to a fishmonger's serenade.... Now it's whistling swans.... And sometimes, from farther waters, choirs of whales."

She settles back in her armchair. Leonardo, the piebald tomcat, jumps onto her lap. She is content with her voices, her cats. And glad for my company once every week or so.

Then she jumps up, spilling Leonardo and her untouched tea, gathers her splattered smock from its hook, her palette and paints from the kitchen.

"Swans — that's what I need for the moats. And a whale for the bay beyond. It's gotten so overcast outside, would you mind shining that light there — just bend its neck — so I can see what I'm doing. Almost out of white paint — could I trouble you to bring me a tube next week?"

I jot "White Paint" in my notebook. I'm forgetful of late, if I don't write down....

"Now, child, I don't want to detain you. You have a long drive to Richmond, and you had better be on your way before it snows again. Take those cookies for the road. There, in the Louis Sherry tin."

I look in the pantry. Among shoe boxes marked: BRUSHES, CHARCOAL, MARINE FOSSILS (SCALLOPS), MARINE FOSSILS (ANCIENT CLAMS), SHEEP SKULLS, ARROW HEADS, the tin is empty. I write "Fig Newtons" on my list. When I was six, she taught me to arrange them into castles and battlements, as if they were dominos.

Given how the cats are scratching, I add "Flea Powder."

Knowing I might be visiting, the social worker phones. "Good news! Your aunt finally leads the waiting list for the Home. Could be a matter of only a week, at worst two, until...."

Until another resident dies and frees up a bed. Until we — I — must face packing her up. Just the essentials that might survive institutional laundering. The rest will be locked up here until the fate of the place is settled. What of her half-finished canvases stacked in the chicken house? And the cats?

"Is that big ol' house warm enough?" the social worker asks cheerily. "How's your aunt doing?"

"Great," I answer. "And she likes it cool. Let's let her stay here a bit longer. Someone else in more desperate need for a bed can take her place. If necessary, I can get leave from work for a few weeks."

Even years.... Since I'm supposed to inherit this farm, I'd better get used to staying here in season and out. Until one morning they discover me collapsed in the barn, or drowned in the inlet, or shrivelled and stiff in this wildly painted parlor, even with brushes dried in my hands. That's the way to go, Aunt Eleanora has said.

I thank the social worker, hang up.

"Next weekend," I promise Aunt Eleanora, "rain or shine, I'll drive you around to see horses. And if the weather should be warm — it will be spring soon — I'll walk you down to the cove, and we'll feed some crusts to the ducks. I could even push you in a wheelchair all the way up the path to the lighthouse."

Preoccupied with outlining her swans, she seems not to pay attention.

I tape another sheet of plastic over a broken pane, then bank the fire, raise the thermostat, go outside with a broomstick to check the level of heating oil. Will that be enough to last until April? She has enough food in the fridge to last the week, a cupboard of cans, as well as the cauldron of chicken I've got simmering on her old iron stove. Afraid she'll forget it, I cut the flame: she doesn't mind lukewarm soup, and the house is always cold enough so it won't spoil. I wash and refill bowls with food for the anxious cats.

What would happen to them?

In a corner of the kitchen counter I notice a bag of crusts and stale bread. Although the weather has been too cold for her to venture outside, she still intends to walk down to the inlet to feed the wild ducks. Despite all her cats, there is evidence the mice from the walls are taking their share of crumbs along the way. She won't let anyone buy traps or poison.

The first flurries of snow. I run to the inlet with the bag of crusts, past the broken skiff caught in the ice rimming the shore. Can still see some red and blue paint where Jeff and I painted the hull, then added a squiggly blue waterline, like waves, which Great Uncle Ramsey warned was ridiculous, but we were twelve or thirteen.

Two mallards are paddling among the waves beyond the ice. I fling the crusts. The ducks skid across to retrieve them.

"More crusts next week, I promise you."

Suddenly I freeze as twenty whistling swans fly in line. They fracture the sun, then veer so low the tips of their wings skim the water like skipping stones. One swan breaks formation, swerves from the others, lands in the cove. At last the rest follow. They reach their long necks underwater to forage for seaweed and softshell clams, until the water is tufted by triangles of upended swans.

When I stop in the house to gather up my computer and Aunt Eleanora's laundry, and to say goodbye, I hear her humming. A whale is swimming into life among the galleons in the sea between the tall clock and the fireplace.

I tiptoe out, load the car, give it a few minutes to warm up.

The whole drive to town, the humming persists.

WORKING THE CLAY

She is showing an ancient way to make pots. She needs no wheel, only damp clay on a platform of stone.

The sun bursts between boulders: already the morning is warm. The pine which gave her shade for seventy years is dead.

She is rib-thin and wrinkled, her fingers crimped, braids gray.

The mass of clay weighs too much to lift, but she flattens the base: the pot will be large.

A man, also the color of clay, brings pails of water, more clay. She does not seem to notice.

He chops the pine into logs. Other people approach, sit in a circle.

An eagle rises to split the sky.

She gropes for more clay, rolls it into a snake, encircling the base with gritty flesh. More snakes blend as she smooths them, coil higher and higher, walling the base.

The sun is beginning to singe.

It takes time. She works slowly. The man offers water. She shakes her head. She alone does not sweat. The others wander away to the shade.

She fills her pipe with peculiar leaves, lights them and draws bitter smoke.

The lower wall is already firm. She adds ever more coils. The pot swells its circular belly.

She seems tired, but continues to knead the clay into snakes into walls. She can no longer reach the rim. The man lifts her up toward the sun, lowers her gently into the pot. He stands outside, handing her fistfuls of clay. From inside, she increases the number of circles.

Only her hands are visible now, and wisps of smoke.

The neck of the pot narrows like an amphora.

The man tests the sides, kneads the last lump of clay, flattens it over a rock, lifts the sagging platter-like mass over the pot. Her fingers reach up to receive it. Together they center the lid. From outside he seals all the edges.

Wiping sweat and clay from his face, he squats in the shade of the pot, watches the slant of the sun. By sunset the clay seems dry.

At last he arranges pine logs, charcoal and twigs, then piles stones in a ring arching upward into a dome.

The others return to watch flames through chinks between stones. The kiln glows all night.

At sunrise the embers are grey.

THE WRECK OF THE KATIE MAE

They're taking away our boat.

Not "ours." Some hapless oysterman's Katie Mae. One flood tide, full moon at the equinox, she broke from a distant mooring, floated over the shoals. Or a squall sped her hurtling across the river under bare poles. Hurricane Agnes, in '72? Or that big one September of '38, before they tagged disasters with feminine names.

Whenever, she beached herself on our spit of cattails and sand, western edge of Nan's Cove near the marker dividing channel from shallows. With every tide and storm, her keel digs deeper into our marsh.

A peeling hulk of a rotting hull, windshield from the gaping bridge smashed and catching light in the bilge, engine rusted apart in the hold, winches frozen, pump snapped in three but rainwater drains between planks where caulking crumbles to sand.

Old bag lady escaped from the poorhouse, she never was a Rockette of a racing yacht nor princess clipper fallen on hard times, only a staunch fishwife of a working boat who took the seas without rolling too far. She lugged bushels of oysters dusted with snow, bluefish autumn and spring, in summer blue crabs and clams.

Generations of children, like me, have raced across fields and clumped through the marsh or waded ashore by the sandbar, climbed over splintery gunwales. Skirting the holes on her deck, we set sail around the globe in our buccaneer brigantine, the stout-hearted Katie Mae.

"She'll outlast us all," we said.

Today the State, represented by Mr. Kenvill McCray (Piledriver, Builder of Bulkheads, Jetties and Piers), with his rusty maroon floating crane is hoisting her up from her sandy berth onto a barge. Pieces of keel pull away like scabs.

I didn't know he was there until, out to count swans, I paddled around the point in our green canoe, leaky bow just re-fibreglassed against February waves. All the swans must have been scared away by the giant tongs clutching the hull.

"I love this boat!" I call out. "Please leave her here."

"It's a State Riparian matter," he answers. "We can't let all these derelicts sit rotting their bottoms, breaking apart in storms, cluttering up the shore."

"Old Katie's ridden out decades of storms without falling apart much more than she already has. Herons fish off her stern, ospreys nest on her mast, swallows under her bow. They'll fly back mid-March and search about — "

"That's why we'll get her out before March: don't want to disturb any nests. And these wrecks cover the spots where worms and other tiny aquatic creatures breed in the marsh."

He doesn't look like a man who would care about wiggly things in the briny muck.

I point out she's well above high tide line. "Just heave her farther up on our shore — I like her rotting peacefully here."

"Sorry, ma'am, she belongs to the State once the owner refused to reclaim her. Cheaper to buy a new boat than repair this wreck. And she's sat here for years."

"But where do you plan to take her," I ask, "the Marine Museum downriver?"

"I tow 'em just to the oyster house. Tomorrow the

truck will haul her to the landfill dump up the road."

There archaeologists in the future might pry away enduring layers of trash, bed springs, chassis, bottles, plastics, and cans, to uncover this fossil not quite dissolved in the bog.

I choke back the salt of my anger, don't tell him that back on a hummock among the reeds lies another wreck. Only a skiff, but her ribs will outlast his own, and mine.

And while he's busy securing his prize, I edge my canoe close to his tug, get out my marlin spike. Takes a while, but I pry just enough caulking out of the seams under his waterline...

TIDAL CONFLICTS

I. Making Good Neighbors

Bring me no more Christmas cookies, apple cakes or mint routed from your flower beds. (My shady yard grows only ivy, hooking up my walls.)

You know why I'm angry. Could I mask my wrath under normal politeness — vital for neighbors who share one driveway and years of each other's kids.

You burrow among a stack of bricks on my side. From my study I hear stone against brick, metal on brick. I glance from the window.

"Oh, would you like those old...?"

You scream, "I've cornered the snake!"

"Wait!" I rush out the door. "Let me catch him, I'll set him free in the country Sunday."

Whether you wish to prove your bravado, Laocoön wrestling serpents, or just want the impostor out of the way to spare or to spite me; by the time I arrive, you are pressing a spade against the asphalt with all your might — on a black snake the size of an earthworm.

Symmetrically severed, the front half is long as the piece left behind the spade you finally raise.

I pick up the halves, both bleeding, both undulating. The onyx head is banded pale gold, the tongue flickers as if to explore its new situation. Who knows how aware one end is of the other, uncoiled.

Whatever I shout in my outrage, you defend your act by claiming your daughter is "phobic."

"Nonsense!" I mutter. "You must have instilled her fear."

"I don't care for snakes," you admit.

Nor for most creatures: Your daughter comes

over to play with our kittens. I'd have taught her, black snakes are harmless, they do good, the mother snake surely ate those rats who rampaged through your garbage.

"Wildlife in a city should be preserved."

"Snakes make her phobic," you repeat, as if they were strawberries causing a rash. "Since she saw this one here three days ago, she's not slept. In her nightmares he swallows her up."

I almost suggest: You should both go to shrinks.

Granted, some people hate animals: the word snake sends Paul into shivers, John goes insane at one glimpse of a cat. And I hate wasps.

One sorrowful half of a tiny snake in each hand, I retreat, release them among my ivy. Could the head segment survive?

"Next time you find any animal call me."

And I go in my house to pack for the country.

II. Ito Jakuchu, artist, b. 1716, in Kyoto

I imagine him as a boy at his father's market rearranging radishes long and white, like albino carrots, in patterns with scarlet ones, as if stones in temple courtyards. He piles melons high as the mountains beyond the market, polishes squashes, loquats and ginger roots, shakes rain from bouquets of green onions, and his small fingers stroke the gills of shitake mushrooms so lightly they leave no mark but come away fragrant with rotting oak.

His father cannot trust him to guard the poultry: he might unhinge bamboo cages to free the ducks. He has released roosters into the snow before, scattered good grain in a heap so they stay pecking there long enough for him to sketch tail plumes' darkgreen fire, manes' iridescent bronze, proud heads with rubbery wattles.

And in lulls between serving housewives with baskets, fishermen with seaweed to trade for spinach, farmers bartering rice for salt, is he drawing chrysanthemums in the dirt, or with a charcoal lump covering boards with swirls and birds and bamboo, prefiguring his colors on rice paper and silk edged with brocade, scrolls so precious the temple priests hid them away from the eyes of peasants, fishermen, vendors of fruit.

He would understand why I apologize to the tomato before my knife slices, and caress the plumage of the tawny hen while I wait for the stew pot to boil.

III. A Wound-up Cat Always Runs in a Circle Through Snow

Somewhere there is always blood in the snow, somewhere a mouse on the run in spite of his wounds, just ask the cat floating over his brain in circles —

This grey mouse now in my palm encircled (after I tried and tried, always in vain, to help him escape), held in a napkin damask as snow, white belly up, ears trembling, pink front paws running, hind legs paralyzed by a wound in the tiny spine from the teeth of the cat who, acting out the essence of cat encircling her prey, the nature of hunter always lurking under her gossamer fur, noticed him slip in from the snow, saw him run, skitter on toothpick legs over the floor like a wound-up toy zipping around the living room until he wound down as if the battery inside were tired.

But the cat, tireless, chased him in circles, breaking them only to snatch him up, always right before he broke out of range of her snow-soft paws since she is too plump to run fast, then she dropped him to watch him run again, flecks of blood from wounds dotting his fur and the licked teeth of the cat who has not yet disturbed the circuitous innards.

So he remains live but always more terrified, forgetting the snowstorm which drove him indoors, the snowy thin ring around his black eyes running invisible tears from the wound also to his psyche as the long-nightmared image of cat ensnares him in the narrowing circle of the evening's reality which always was crouching here as it always is....

And stepping out in the snow — since his motor still runs there's a chance his wounds might heal — I leave him, come in to the cat already asleep in her furry circle.

IV. Evidence

Yesterday's snow clings to our boots, drifts into furrows of turnips and kale, winter wheat stretching down to the beach patterned by claws and webbed feet.

"Damn it, look, right off our shore: a blind — "

"And decoys."

A flotilla of stiff-winged boards dappled grey or black. Strung out, they spin askew like bathtub toys. What goose would be fooled.

Who the hell rowed here in our absence, beached his boat, broke our trees, pounded those stakes, nailed a frame of sticks camouflaged with our cattails and weeds?

Below the tide line, a beach is no-man's land. Everyman's sea.

We stumble over the stag. One antler snapped off: for a souvenir? The other horn branches into the sand like roots of a hapless tree.

"Was he killed upriver, then washed ashore a few tides ago?"

"But prints lead from the marsh to the beach, stop at the hooves."

"Or was he shot in the woods, then hobbled across the fields to find water?"

"But the river is briny and he'd have passed the pond."

"He was shot here," I say, "Point-blank by whoever built that blind."

I phone the sheriff.

"Sure, we'll stop by next week, if we can find your road. But everyone round here hunts."

Meanwhile, on the beach, the stag lies stiff, decoys jerk in the waves, and before dawn the hunter again rows across in his skiff.

V. Swan Story

You kept hounding me, as we lay in the feathered bed: "Now write something important."

So I went out to write on the man who shot down whistling swans, while I stood alone on the bluff overlooking the frozen cove, my boots soaked with slush, mittens too thin, and how I'd shot him (simpler to shoot down a man than a startled bird), but I was so quick he'd no time to be startled, he dropped in the snow on the beach reddening like the swan.

And no one who has seen swans in flight or floating over the waves or parading on ice too thin for a man, or heard all night in the inlets and bays their woo-ho woo-woo woo-ho or however the bird books try in vain to describe their flutes and whistles and cries, no one who knows swans would dispute that mine was a crime of passion, a gesture of self-preservation.

You, also, love swans, would lie to provide me with alibis.

So I buried the gun in a woodchuck hole, then, retracing my way through the snow, dragged a branch over my tracks, brought it home to add to the fire, and sat down to write my story for you.

But you said, " Where have you been out there all this time in the cold. It's already dark, you are soaked and spoiling the rug, come to bed with me get warm — "

So I never got to my story at all.

Next week I will, if the swans have flown back to the cove.

VI. Catfishing

When I slash the catfish, you look terribly shocked. I'm told you are hung like an elephant: did castration flash into your head?

The children hauled the oyster basket up to the dock dripping seaweed and two huge catfish, whiskered giants who haunt the nightmares of tadpoles and grace dreams of those fishermen who can nail the broad head to a board, slit quickly around, peel the skin like a sock or a condom away.

You refuse to clean any fish.

No hammer or nails.

My knife is silver and small, but it cuts. I grasp that live head with a flowered towel, avoiding the spines, rows of teeth, gash, and wish for pliers, cleavers, your help.

You stand there, aghast at guts. But the children admire life rebelling, persisting, fetch the pail to rinse the filets.

You like my catfish stew, and later make a proposition, but I turn you down.

VII. Preparing the Feast

The old French cookbook told us how to fix our eels: slit round the neck, slip off the skin, and slice.

But how to hold these whips which switch from lash to hoop to question mark even when our pliers, scissors, knives have stripped the slimy skin away?

We cut their bellies, tear out guts. They'll stop this senseless squirming now, and die.

Still they flail, alive as when ,our hands so close, we pried them off your hook.

How soon would they have undulated off to breed in the Sargasso Sea? We can't.

The butter sizzles. I must grasp one eel. He gasps. I look away. You press your knife. At last it crunches through the vertebrae. The head slides in the sink. Slices twitch.

Next the second eel.

Our sides touch, and we move apart.

The bluegrey flesh cooks gold. Add garlic, wine, parsley, salt, spinach, dill. We turn to clean the sink.

Those heads are live! They quiver, puff their cheeks, their lips pose questions, they answer with their eyes. Heads edge close. Mouths press a kiss as chaste as ours must be....

We eat *anguilles au vin,* still out of touch.

VIII. Dinnertime

Fresh out of chicken backs to bait the trap in the cove, I used broken clams and small frozen spot caught off the island Fourth of July. This smorgasbord never lures as many crabs, but last night a young she-crab, in search of safe haven to shed her tight exoskeleton, edged through the jagged gap in the lower tier of the chicken-wire cage, and a big jimmy followed.

Sex and food go hand in claw. I watched him nibble the final bit of fish through the smaller mesh of the bait compartment. She in turn grabbed a mandible full of clam just for fortification before they got down to business.

I, who don't like to eat land creatures, now buy a yellow styrofoam tray of chicken backs at the SuperFresh, extract one ivory-skinned sunset-fleshed maroon-boned hunk.

I cross the fields to the dock, haul up the rope. There, coupled in a corner of cage, are the newly-shed she-crab and the hard-shelled male. His plated claws embrace her with what, among crabs, may stand for tenderness.

Four stalked eyes watch me — with fear? Annoyance? Greed? Too anthropomorphic. At least a primitive interest: could I serve as dessert? I thrust the chicken not in the bait holder but in the main cage near the crabs who hunch and clutch.

I lower the trap with what among humans passes for care into the briny water again. When they're done, may they feast, the way we, after a similar act, gorge ourselves strong again on caviar and oysters, or the Romans on peacocks and antelope steaks.

I'll wait until evening, then like Caesar Tiberius or

Caligula (knives in the spines of cousins and friends) and other hypocrites from ancient Rome to this farm by the Chesapeake, while admiring their ardor and armor I too will betray, seize my tired prey from behind. To keep up the sea's population, I'll free the female, her paper-shell carapace shielding new roe, but drop the jimmy into my basket.

Then we, scavengers too, will edge ourselves into bed.

SORTING LAUNDRY

Folding clothes, I think of folding you into my life.

Our king-sized sheets like table cloths for the banquets of giants, pillow cases, despite so many washings seams still hold our dreams.

Towels patterned orange and green, flowered pink and lavender, gaudy, bought on sale, reserved, we said, for the beach, refuse, even after years, to bleach into respectability.

So many shirts and skirts and pants recycling week after week head over heels recapitulate themselves.

All those wrinkles to be smoothed, or else ignored, they're in style.

Myriad uncoupled socks went paired into the foam like those creatures in the ark.

And what's shrunk is tough to discard even for Goodwill.

In pockets, surprises: forgotten matches; lost screws clinking on enamel; paper clips, whatever they held between shiny jaws, now dissolved or clogging the drain; well-washed dollars, legal tender for all debts public and private, intact despite agitation; and gleaming in the maelstrom, one bright dime; a broken necklace of good gold you brought from Kuwait.

The strangely tailored shirt left by a former lover...

If you were to leave me, if I were to fold only my own clothes, the convexes and concaves of my blouses, panties, stockings, bras turned upon themselves, a mountain of unsorted wash could not fill the empty side of the bed.

OCTOBER LETTER

I've tried it too many times with husbands and lovers when they've insisted: Quit writing, finish the dishes, pay bills, and what do *you* know about writing plays? Or they admitted "literature" bored them.

I've abandoned characters caught in the midst of an act, stranded between chapter or verse. Some are wandering still, waiting out there, frozen to statues, crickets crawling across their legs.

Now you remind me: Time to put in storm windows, scythe those weeds, paint the porch.

Which means: Swear off writing again.

Yet this is October. Flat calm. A natural time for limitation. Ospreys have flown, geese and swans not yet settled down.

Mice already move into the larder, test half-packets of crackers behind the neighbors' gift of strawberry wine. Their harvester stripped the soy bean field, destroyed the blackberry patch which filled my pails last July.

Milkweed pods rattle among thickets of stick-tight burrs. Puffballs explode in the meadows. Frost blackens basil, lawns fade. Tomatoes, green in a tangle of ragweed, must redden indoors.

Still, I'll bait the traps off the pier, though most crabs have scuttled toward deeper channels.

I also should. And should bail rain from the boat. I still do what I ought, and ought not. Or at least, write about it.

Though I grow older, I've not yet run out of excuses. Have become more inventive.

Not one pad of paper. Only your note: *Fridge Needs To Be Cleaned.*

I erase it with care, outline Scene III.

The lawn bursts with autumnal crocus. And the wind's coming up —

I bail the boat, and set sail.

HUNTERS' MOON
OR
HOW I WENT OUT TO HUNT THE HUNTERS

The first shots rang out as I was thinning the turnip greens. Not that I'm crazy about turnips, but what do you plant mid-September when pumpkins overwhelm two-thirds of the garden and you've already sown curly kale, broccoli and albino radishes? Turnips by the silvery moon. Not on the advice of any almanac, but as I rototilled August's weeds under the final third and scattered tiny round seeds from an anonymous brood-mare of a turnip, the moon rose fresh from the cove beyond the soybean field.

Two more shots from beyond the beans. Better not be from our side of the cove.

I rent only this ramshackle farmhouse by the Chesapeake, but feel proprietary about all ninety acres the landlord plants in tobacco, corn and soybeans. I plastered NO HUNTING signs on a dozen trees around the periphery. Highly visible. Evidently ineffectual.

One more volley, and Singa, the fluffy tawny tomcat stalking toads among marigolds, dashes into the cornfield.

October's first strings of geese honk low over the cove. With luck they'll land on these fields tonight. Full moon tonight. Harvest moon. Hunters' moon.

No moon last night. Rain. Only a lull now. The clothes on the line are sopping, including my embroidered dress from Crete. Must iron it for Baltimore day after tomorrow.

If the car is working. I'll find out *if* the car is working *if* the phone is working. The phone may work *if* it stops raining. Also *if* it stops raining, the bedroom ceiling may stop leaking.

Because of the leaks, last night I had to sleep on the pull-out couch downstairs.

In droughty August, which I mentioned was a good season for roof repairs, the landlord grinned, "Ain't leaking now."

Outdoors work he's not lazy about. Half the reason I took this place was the jungle of plum trees, mulberry shrubs and blackberry vines enshrouding the house. But when I arrived to take my ephemeral possession, he had bushhogged and chopped everything down. Only the vines have had time to regrow.

Last March the landlord ploughed the garden for me, in exchange for the Nouveau Beaujolais which Tom, a would-be lover, brought down but we never got to opening because his kids wanted Cokes so we rowed across the cove to the bait-and-tackle and he bought beer too. The landlord tractored his discs over this rectangle, ripped through turf and stone-strewn stone-hard soil as if through sand. I rototilled, fertilized, planted old tubers and new seeds.

The garden exploded asparagus, Jerusalem artichokes, spinach, lettuce, tomatoes, squashes, herbs. And bugs and weeds. At least autumn crops are spared bugs, weeds.

I'm thinning turnip greens for supper. My former husbands disliked turnips, and their greens. I may tire of them too. But except for what guests bring, all summer I've lived off garden, sea and berry patches, and must somehow continue.

The scabby apples from the arthritic tree suit only applesauce.

All summer my traps caught four to six hard-shells

a day. Sometimes a newly-shed crab too. Surplus crab meat and softshells I've frozen for winter. Papershells, the recently shed but already crackly, by law I must release to harden and grow and shed again.

By now most surviving crabs have scuttled toward deep water, burrowed into the bottom for winter. Still, yesterday I stuffed fish heads into the crabpots tied to the pier. Before sunset I'll check: if not crabs, perch and eel sometimes swim through the funnels. Wish bluefish were as effortless to catch.

Summer dwindling, weekend guests won't often venture down with their steaks and cakes and Cokes.

Without distractions, I'll finish more translations faster. I usually express the finished draft back, but a client in Baltimore wants me to come in to discuss a new project. And Tom...

If the car...

More shots. Two at once. One double-barrelled shotgun? Or two men with single-barrelled shotguns firing simultaneously? How close? Sound travels differently in different weathers. From the cove? Or from the hedgerow separating this land from the Bryants. Mrs. B, eighty, crochets afghans and sells honey. Her sons come down the peninsula weekends to check their hives and work their fields. And, "when deer become a nuisance," they hunt. On their side of the hedge-row.

Last June I often surprised fawns playing on both sides of the hedgerow. Now they're grown: fair game.

Am I, too?

More shots. Close together, yet don't sound the same. Different kinds of rifles?

I oppose hunting. I continue opposing as I crouch over the turnips. That's how I protest much I dislike in this world: by keeping my head low over my garden.

A wise course, when opposing firearms. I'm not always wise.

Friday I sat on the sun porch, typing translations of Greek business clippings for a New York firm. My third-hand Hyundai in the shop, nothing indicated anyone home. Nor did I expect visitors. Few find this farm, off a tertiary county road where the mailbox is rusted through, then a mile down a lane pocked with puddles guests complain almost swallow their cars. Those who ignore my map go astray. Even the bottled-gas truck misses the turn.

Friday, however, my first visitors were Jehovah's Witnesses. They bumped down this road to offer their leaflet "How Angels Affect Our Lives."

"Amazing what you're doing with this old place," the first Witness beamed.

"Haven't you painted ...?" began Witness Two. "I'd love to look sometime."

Cobwebs weave together the corners of rooms, tatters blow over the porch, basil and lavender dry over curtain rods, and though Asian-style I discourage shoes worn indoors, still dust and sand seep inside.

I accepted their leaflet but postponed tours. I'll wait for angels.

Friday afternoon, hearing a heavy vehicle, I thought the landlord had come to cut his corn. So tall and thick you lose yourself, though now dry beige stalks rattle skeletons in the wind. Ears are heavy and hard, interlocking rows of golden pebbles to feed hogs.

An unfamiliar blue pickup bounced off the dirt road and parked by the barn. Two men in camouflage fatigues climbed down.

"Hello," I called. "Are you lost?"

"No, ma'am, just gonna shoot us a few doves."

"Great season for doves." Settling an iridescent orange hat on his dark hair, the other man took two shotguns from the dusty truck. "And deer."

"Oh, sorry, didn't you see my signs? No hunting here. Too many children." I swept my hand toward the house, as if it would burst forth rumbles of toddlers.

"We'll be way over in the corn."

The first man swept his arm toward the cove.

"I'm afraid the landlord absolutely refuses to allow anyone to hunt on his property."

The landlord heads the county hunt. In red coats, tan jodhpurs and velvet helmets they hoist themselves onto horses, charge off like the Light Brigade. No firearms, only beagles. He swears they've never caught a fox.

The men leaned against their pickup, fondling shotguns, chewing tobacco, or gum, like cud. No angels these.

In childhood I always lost the game of Stare Down, blinking or giggling before my opponent.

I glared those men in the eye for a ripe minute. Finally they turned, climbed in the truck, backed around, creased tire marks across lawn and garden, disappeared up the road.

I won, that day.

Suppose I hadn't. As Tom said on the phone, "Dumb thing for a woman to dispute armed men. And without wheels for a quick retreat. When'll your car be fixed?"

On blocks, my car awaits some unique screw for the transmission. "They don't stock foreign parts in this county," explained Joe, the blond-bearded, long-haired mechanic.

Joe drove me home with my staples: bread-flour, brown sugar, milk and eggs from the IGA store. From Feed & Seed, Kibbles for Singa and cracked corn for geese. We stopped at the roadside stand for Concord grapes, first and last of the season. Expensive. Beloved.

Granted rent's lower here than my old Baltimore apartment, resuscitating a *circa*-1900 farmhouse means ripping through money like bluefish chomping through mullet. Moving in mid-March before water or electricity were connected, I scraped stained peach-pink and scaly lime-green wallpaper, then guests helped paint downstairs walls snow-white, ceilings blue as Grecian skies. When the landlord patches the roof, I'll paint upstairs.

The kitchen floor, patched ocher surface worn to the bone, heaves from unseen mighty roots, like the shifting of tectonic plates, and creates gullies and ridges like horsts and grabens. Desertscape. New blue linoleum remains rolled in the closet until someone —

More shooting. Geese break V's, flap wildly, but, I believe, escape. How many dead doves/ducks/deer? Pity doves and ducks and deer can't turn around like tigers, sharks and polar bears, and eat their hunters.

Crows in the oak.

A second string of geese bays its way downriver. With luck they'll avoid these fields today.

Shots resound oddly, clouds distort sound, noise bounces off obstacles. But now shots reverberate — from behind the barn?

Or the magnolia? House-high, room-wide, roof-thick, branches bend and take root, new saplings sprout, stretch and entangle. The banyan canopy could shelter a platoon. Branches brush against the house like hungry moose.

Are those the same hunters? Stray shots, stray hunters. Everyone must be hunting today.

Raining again, but lightly. I abandon the colander of turnip greens, park my sneakers and soggy socks on the back porch, retreat indoors. The kitchen is redolent with grapes in silver bowls and basil in the silver pitcher. Saturday Tom and his children came. They insist they love to visit. I sense, however, they aren't at home in the country. Always some emergency of cut feet because they won't wear shoes on the farm, or something floats away because they don't think about the tide.

Tom comes right back with the argument, "Way out here, babe, what would you do in an emergency?"

What would I do in an emergency? Potential weapons are: 1) dull kitchen knives; 2) a two-handled scythe, 50-100 years old, found in the barn, needs a whetstone; 3) one BB gun. Douglas bought it to shoot at tin cans, then used it on pigeons. When he returned to Oklahoma for what turned out to be seven years and an easier separation than imagined, so easy that neither of us quarrelled, he left me the BB gun along with our apartment, also easy to leave. Now the BB gun is stashed in the closet behind the new linoleum.

What's one BB gun against shotguns? Provocative. You don't attack superior forces head-on, Niko, my first husband, claimed. "In guerrilla warfare, as in love, be ingenious."

Suppose this were a war, enemy landing in the cove, slogging marshes, filtering hedgerows, commandoing across fields, seizing barns, and here I'm holding — my fort.

The original farmhouse, shown on an old map, was built about 1670. When the British sailed the Chesapeake in the War of 1812, they destroyed it. Subsequent houses burned or collapsed, and in 1889 this was built on old foundations. Rooms, amenities and dependencies were added on so the structure humps out under its quilts of wisteria and honeysuckle.

The cellar floor is mud, the retaining walls flat stones with mud between, recent sections rough concrete. Yesterday, when the temperature dropped, I went downstairs to examine the dinosaur furnace. Singa padded ahead and to my astonishment found a second stone staircase sealed off under the kitchen. When? Why? Like an amputated limb it maintains a ghostly existence.

If the enemy destroyed the house, this cellar would serve as bunker. Crouched on the stairs, one could fire muskets, shotguns, machine guns, BBs.

In my childhood, BB shot came in cylinders the size of penny rolls or fly-paper, or by the pound in bags. Today's come in cartons as for cream. Mysteriously, spontaneously, BBs roll out beneath the cellar door, trickle into corners, skid under baseboards beyond any broom. Maybe mice kick them out because barefoot I step —

More shots, from far, from close by. Hunters still around. And shouldn't be.

So much for BBs. That's one gun that won't fire today. For protection, try garden clippers, or a hoe.

"In emergencies," the landlord suggested, "call the sheriff."

I wrote that number by the plumber's, doctor's, electrician's. Are they taking this afternoon off to hunt too?

The sheriff hunts. Everyone in the county hunts, the landlord says, just like his daddy, granddad, great granddad on back and Indians before them. Nowadays a few bleeding-heart city liberals act finicky about guns, while here, yes, great season for everything.

More shooting. I retie my muddy shoes, grab my yellow rain-slicker.

Hunters might still mistake me for a deer. As Joe says, "Every fall some fool —"

Not that I'm afraid, but best alert them I'm coming. And warn any bird or deer dumb enough to be hanging around. A boom-box!

The batteries in the portable radio are corroded.

Had I a drum, or tambourine, I'd bang it the way

Japanese priests bless a house, or Chinese mourners beat gongs at funerals to scare evil spirits, or encourage the departing soul to get on with it. The way beaters walk noisily ahead to flush game so hunters can shoot it.

The way church bells — Bells!

One wooden bell. Niko got it in Indonesia when we stopped between Athens and Los Angeles. This bell hung around the neck of the only black-brown-and-white cow in the herd, other cows were dustbeige or white. I take it from its hook in the living room. A cool hollow sound. Too quiet.

One small vaguely conical iron bell hangs by the back door. From Niko's grandmother's donkey. Rusty tinkle.

Finally, one cowbell, so heavy it must be meant for a bull. Coppery inside, rusted exterior. Rectangular, pyramidic, five inches by four by five-and-one-half, from who knows where. Found near the well, the only item left by former tenants, its hefty clang alerts someone on the beach there's a phone call.

Nobody on the beach today. No phone today. Were there an emergency, it would be an emergency.

Shots.

I grab the cowbell, stuff a burlap sack in my pocket, head out. Singa, fur glistening rain drops, leaps from the corn. He often follows me. At the first ring of my bell, he pauses. Another volley of shots, another clang: he flicks his plume, vanishes into the barn.

I jog northeast up the lane, past the barn, at the second telephone pole turn southeast toward the cove, the shooting. Edging cornfield and beanfield, I follow tracks overgrown with briars, ragweed, poison ivy. As I run, the bell clangs. Melodiously.

Breathless, I slow down. This is the most ridiculous exercise I ever heard of. If someone came down this road or emerged from the woods, heard me, saw me cantering along ringing a cowbell\bullbell in the rain, they'd think me some kind of nut.

Ostensibly, I'm out to check crabpots. And after all this rain, soon there should be puffballs, fungi fit for the gods.

No shooting for several minutes. The bell may be working. Or the hunters are tired of rain. My slicker leaks.

Now I pad between these fields like an Indian, surprising a great blue heron in the marsh. Suppose the hunters shot a heron? I tramp through fields, feet soaked, then, extracting the long-handled crab net from the honeysuckle and poison ivy, tread warily the slippery planks of the catwalk over the marsh, still ringing, pealing, tolling my strangely joyful noise.

Reaching the makeshift pier where the skiff lies low in the water, I check the pilings. All bare. The first trap is empty. The other holds two big jimmies, crusty granddads, seaweed fuzzing their shells. I dump them on the planks, plant a foot lightly on their backs, grab the hindmost swimming flippers so the claws can't reach me. Into the sack. On shore again, I wipe gunk from the crab pot onto wet grass, but my hands remain gritty grey.

Should row to the bait-and-tackle shop, buy a newspaper, use their phone. Tom asked me to call him about my trip into town, he wants to order tickets for something. Joe said call about the car. And perhaps someone caught surplus bluefish, the gulls are diving like crazy off the point, and me with only this skiff —

Full of rainwater. No point bailing till the rain stops. Falling harder. And dark falls increasingly early.

Shots ring out, a volley, but from the far hedgerow, no longer the landlord's land. The enemy retreats!

Thanks to my bell, or the rain.

I'm shivering. Hair and clothes dripping, sack of crabs swinging from my left hand, bell ringing in my right, I hurry homeward past the barn, hear only crows.

In the garden, I pick up the colander of turnip greens rinsed by the rain. From between the rosemary and parsley I snip three sprigs of mint. Need a cup of hot tea right now. One toe prying the heel of the other foot, I worry off my muddy shoes on the back step.

The kitchen floor! This mud is not mine.

Nor the trail of red leading to the kitchen table.

Nor this man sitting here in duckbill cap, jacket and trousers all of grey/green/beige camouflage material, shotgun in his left hand, right arm wrapped in my embroidered dress — swiped from the clothesline for a bandage. Blood sweeps through, filling in the red cross-stitchery on the white linen, dripping onto the yellow oilcloth.

"Lord — What happened? Raise your arm over your head — Higher — "

He raises both hands, the good arm still clutching his shotgun. The ersatz bandage partly falls away from his wounded arm, but, still holding his hands over his head, he wraps it around his mottled sleeve.

Whatever was it I never learned about pressure points and application of ice —

"I'll get iodine. A doctor." Skimming my list of emergency numbers — plumber, electrician, sheriff, garage — I shift the colander, bell and sack of crabs to the left hand, reach for the phone with my right. I've never tested 911's new system which supposedly automatically pinpoints the caller-in-distress, knows where to send fire engines, ambulances, police.

He waves the shotgun. "Leave that phone alone."

I lift the receiver.

"I don't like iodine or doctors. Drop that phone."

No dial tone anyway. With deliberate deliberation I replace the receiver in its cradle but don't let go, merely stare at him.

Hair, rust-colored, fringes under the camouflage cap, both dark with rain. Something between stubble and brief beard, reddish with patches of grey. Thin face, weathered yet pale around the eyes, must wear sunglasses a lot. Nose thin, tip askew, as if he had lost a fight. Hard to tell his height, sitting, or, given the bulky jacket, his weight. His hands are big, fingers long in proportion to palm, slender, stained with dirt and blood.

He looks at my dirty hands clutching colander, sack, cowbell. Did he hear me ringing it out there? Was he observing me?

He lowers his arms. In his good hand, his left, is his shotgun. He might be left-handed.

An ordinary real-life shotgun, I guess, metal barrel, wooden butt. Shells of red cardboard and brass stud his vest. Nothing metaphorical about that weapon.

"Keep your arm up," I repeat. "It'll prevent the blood from bleeding so fast. Can you press on the wound?"

A "No" grunted through clenched teeth.

I set the bell on the counter, colander and burlap sack in the sink. Running water over the greens activates the crabs who start crawling out. I shove them back in.

"I need some water," he says.

I fill two glasses with cold water, hand him one though I can't remember if accident victims should be given liquids. Approaching, I smell whiskey.

"Just set the glass down." He is clutching the shotgun with his left hand. His bloodied right arm is raised at the elbow. At least when he picks up the glass, he'll have to lay down the gun.

He avoids looking at his arm. So do I.

I drink my glass down. The cold pours down my throat and reminds me I wanted hot tea. I gag as he pulls back a piece of his jacket sleeve, so part of the reddening bandage — the skirt part — falls away from his arm, the rest has stuck. Averting his eyes, he tries to dip the upper side of his forearm in the water glass. His arm is too big, the sleeve interferes, pinkish water overflows.

"Isn't blood supposed to clot better if you don't disturb it," I say. "And that's well water, okay to drink, but should be boiled for medicinal purposes." How prim I must sound, stuffy, with luck even efficient. "What did you do, shoot yourself?"

"No."

Hope he's lying. Otherwise, someone else was — is? — out there with a weapon.

And I was out there ringing my absurd cowbell.

"Caught in barbed wire?"

"Could you boil some water?"

"In a minute."

I have to go upstairs for a minute. First I set the kettle on the stove, turn on the gas. "I'll look what first-aid stuff is in the upstairs bathroom."

He starts to get up.

"Stay seated — you could faint from loss of blood. Keep that arm higher. Press on the wound. I'll get gauze, something clean for bandaging."

Not a time to consider that my dress is ruined. I'm embarrassed I had such a thought. But what will I wear in Baltimore? To pay the security deposit here, I sold most of my city clothes in a yard sale before I moved.

Turning, walking evenly upstairs, I assume he won't shoot me in the back. A shuffling — crabs in the sink, or his feet?

First aid supplies are actually in the kitchen. Statistics indicate — Douglas loved statistics — most accidents happen in kitchens. Upstairs, burrowing in the cabinet, I find what's left of the linen Grandmama handed-me-down for my first wedding. Only she did not disapprove. Sheets, yellowing, disintegrating along old folds, historic. And here's the towel Tom forgot: lavender flowers.

Through the rain-streaked window I see the cat dashing from barn to garden to magnolia. Were someone hiding there....

In the mirror: my mud-streaked face, wet hair, wet muddy clothes.

In the interval the faucet's off, I hear creaking. The rickety kitchen chair?

"You coming back?" the man shouts from downstairs. His accent isn't Southern Maryland. Nothing I can place.

"In a moment."

How to get him to his car, didn't notice his car, can he drive himself to the hospital, seven miles north, if it's a gun wound the sheriff —

Coming downstairs, I tear the sheet into strips. Isn't that what you're supposed to do? His camouflage cap is off. Out of deference to a — lady? Doubtful. His hair is rusty thatch, grey at the temples. How drained his face! His bad arm upright from the elbow, his good hand on the shotgun, he nudges the glass of bloody water.

"Don't worry, we'll get you to the emergency room, somehow. Did you park up our road?"

"Not going to any hospital."

"You must."

"Not that bad."

Then why are you bleeding all over my kitchen?

"You could call your doctor from Mrs. Bryant's up the hill, and the ambulance could pick you up there."

A sudden ironic smile, a grimace. Dear Mrs. Bryant would have a heart attack if she saw him, more likely grab a shotgun herself.

The man keeps glancing at me, at the windows, around the kitchen, through the door into the living room, and back at me. To avoid seeing the bloody glass, his wound?

He also seems to be looking me over. Peculiar activity for a man bleeding to death. He can gauge I'm about five-three in my socks, but given this big slicker, — Niko's — and baggy khakis —Doug's — hard to tell much else.

Even seated, he looks eight feet tall.

We both look about forty.

He has the bluest eyes.

His eyes seem to take in the stereo under its piles of cassettes, Grandmama's silver bowls of scabby green apples and the last glistening Concord grapes, silver pitcher filled with basil, my purse by the phone. My laptop computer is on the sun porch.

Surely he's only a local farmer bent on culling the goose population.

Or an escapee from the Patuxent Prison Farm?

From across the kitchen, my hands full of tatters, I gesture. "Perhaps you'd move that glass — "

He shoves the glass to one side with his elbow. Bloodied water sloshes over the rim, trickles down the oilcloth to the floor. Water and blood soak through the dress and the torn sleeve of his camouflage jacket, darkening, blending with fake jungle colors.

I toss him the flowered towel. "If you'd mop a bit — "

Now he'll have to put down that shotgun.

He doesn't.

The kitchen drawer sticks. Jumbled aspirin, hydrogen peroxide, iodine, ace bandage, tubes of salves whose print is too tiny to read. Magnifying glass, tweezers for splinters, stings. Three Band-Aids and one little square gauze pad, wouldn't cover that arm. No adhesive tape: what did people use before its invention? Snake-bite kit with directions, salve and tiny blades compressed into a rubber thimble like an oversized thumb, supposed to suction venom. Coiled clear plastic tubing attached to a turquoise mouthpiece for reviving the drowned. Better kept in the old icebox by the beach.

The kettle shrieks. I pour boiling water over mint in two teacups, the rest in the big beige bowl. Don't you boil gallons of water for births — at least to keep the prospective father busy?

He mops enough to turn the towel mud-red, lavender flowers purple.

"Now how did you hurt yourself?"

"I didn't — hurt — myself." He grits his teeth.

"Have you got anything to drink?"

"Tea but it needs to steep. One inch of milk left."

He looks insulted. "I mean, something strong. I finished my pint. For warmth."

"The cider's not turned yet. Poor pain-killer anyway." Not the moment to bring out four-star anything. Let him think me a Jehovah's Witness. "Wait for angels."

"Chr-r-rist!"

The crabs overturn the colander and scramble around the sink. Last thing we need is loose crabs. Barefoot, I feel naked. His hiking boots look Size 13.

I tong the crabs into the fridge. The cold will slow them.

Beyond the kitchen window, the sky darkens, rain pings like hail on the stiff magnolia leaves.

"You must see a doctor, get a tetanus shot."

"No, ma'am."

I take a deep breath. "Let's see that arm."

I fold back his sleeve. My dress remains stuck to half the wound.

"Can't you make a tourniquet?" he asks.

"Tourniquets stop bleeding, but you could lose an arm." I forget why. "Better pull off your jacket."

He winces, shifts the shotgun, and holds out his arm. I tug at the cloth.

"Just rip the material."

Garden clippers are in the shed. My manicure scissors, useless for attack or defense, prick through layers of cloth already ripped, the sweater and plaid shirt underneath.

A jagged tear, can't tell how deep. A bullet could have seared it. I thought shotguns fired buckshot. Maybe it wasn't a shotgun. No sign of bullet or shell.

First gunshot wound I've seen. May it be the last. I'd not be much good in a war.

He won't look at the wound, only at me, then out the windows beyond the window seat, toward the tangled magnolia. I dunk his arm awkwardly in the water. He curses.

"Last July a visiting child," I tell him, "a redhead, more red than you, stepped on an oyster shell down on the beach. Tom— the father — got hysterical over the blood, so I drove them both to the emergency room. Tom had to sign all those insurance forms, so I was left with the boy while the Pakistani intern sewed him up. Neat job, but is it true redheads are more sensitive to pain?"

The man is swearing. My chatter is not distracting him. His arm is bleeding. "No iodine."

"Hydrogen peroxide's not supposed to hurt. Do raise your arm. And put down that silly gun."

He doesn't.

I take the brown plastic bottle from the drawer,

struggle to tear the safety wrap with the scissors, to unscrew —

"Darn childproof caps only children can open!"

"Give it here."

Now he'll have to put that gun down. But he holds the bottle in his good hand, bends his head, twists off the cap with his teeth. I pour hydrogen peroxide over the cloth stuck to his wound. It foams all over.

"Goddammittohell, can't you take it easy — God-damn — "

I don't know whether he said "butcher" or "bitch." "Thanks a lot."

"Sorry."

Bubbles of peroxide catch on the pale hairs of his arm, fizz, pop, evaporate.

He glances out the window, then back at me. "Don't worry, I'm not going to shoot you."

"Then get rid of that thing. In real life a shotgun does not have to go off."

"Can't you bandage — this — quickly?" He still hasn't looked at the wound.

"When it dries, we'll squeeze salve on it. Then gauze. I'll wrap it enough in the sheets, tie string around to get the edges of the wound together. My car's in the shop, I'm afraid you'll have to walk up the dirt road to your car."

He almost smiles.

"Thought you said I should sit so I don't faint."

Mint steams the air. I set his cup on the table.

"Honey?"

"Huh?" He looks startled. "Oh. Sure." He settles the shotgun in the crook of his left arm.

Shuffling around the first-aid drawer, I hold the magnifying glass to the tubes. One salve for poison ivy, another for eye infections, a third for burns. How to spread salve on an open wound...?

"There's spray-on Bactine down by the beach, in the old icebox where we store sodas." And beer.

Excuse to go outside, despite the rain, or use the rain for cover, slip off in the twilight, up the hill, from Mrs. Bryant's call the ambulance, the sheriff. Hers is the nearest house, a mile up the hill, an old white house festooned with those afghans and antimacassars she crochets for church bazaars. If she's out, several houses up the road must have phones, 911 can find....

Everyone's phone may be dead.

I could run through the fields to the pier, bail the skiff, row to the bait-and-tackle. Even if their phone's out too, even in weather like this, watermen drop in for tobacco or a pint, someone will call a doctor, someone will recognize him, someone will get him out of here.

Hard to row in this weather, wind pushes the bow off course, but I'll pole with the crab net, hug the shore until I must cross the channel.

"I'll get my slicker."

"You stay right here," the man says. Then: "I'll go with you."

I look at him with dismay. Through the dimming light, the skin above his beard seems to fade measurably paler.

"Let's wrap that arm first — "

He pulls himself up, stands well over six feet. Yet even if he couldn't row, were he in the stern, his weight would steady the skiff.

He takes a step forward, pauses. Then he wobbles, steadies himself, topples. I jump aside, but he grazes me and crashes on the kitchen floor.

Chr-r-rist! Out cold.

I don't own smelling salts. Ammonia's supposed to revive people as well as soothe mosquito bites, bee stings, jellyfish tentacles. Should I dump a bucket of water over his head? Did he hit his brow going down

— a cut I didn't notice before.

First, while he lies there, I hide his shotgun behind the linoleum and BB gun in the closet. The way the spouse of an alcoholic hides bottles. Or an alcoholic hides bottles.

While he's unconscious, this is also the moment to smear salve on a pad of gauze, the stuff for eye infections should be mild enough for a wound still oozing, no time to run outside for the Bactine. Then apply pressure, wrap the torn sheet, or maybe it's then apply pressure? Whichever, quickly before he wakes.

What if he's dead already?

I press on the wound. He twists and moans. Propping the arm, I bind strips of sheet right over the dress.

Now I'll head up the hill, jog, run, call doctors, ambulance, sheriff —

What if he were to die on my floor?

Elevate feet, it said somewhere, so blood doesn't waste time in legs but keeps circulating around head and torso. Baltimore and Washington Yellow Pages and Directories fit under his boots. Muddy. Loosen laces. I open the ammonia, kneel, hold the bottle by his nose. Nothing happens. Maybe I don't want to revive him so quickly.

After inscrutable moments, he writhes around, eyes screwed up, he is gasping, coughing, swearing, suddenly he flails both arms in the air, hunches up, kicks out.

Next thing I know he's whopped my face and I fall against the sink.

He is saying something. I reopen one eye. We are both on the floor, he against the stove, I against the cabinet under the sink. We squint around, cursing each other and our respective pain. Pain is technicolor. Scene from a Grade-C cops-and-robbers melodrama.

I know better than to touch an injured animal.

When Singa got a briar in his paw, I wrapped him in a straightjacket of old towels, and still he scratched me.

Should've left this cat comatose, gotten the hell away. Why didn't I tie him to something. Sure. Untie my shoelace, the string from the linoleum, bind him to the fridge? Stick paring knives through his ribs?

"Keep your arm up."

My fingers touch my face, come away red. Perhaps the metal zipper tab on his jacket caught my cheek. I scramble up, bend over the sink. Water hurts.

"What the — " The man looks wildly around and grabs his arm, which promptly bleeds through the sheet, "Where the — What — "

"You fainted and you hit me."

"Jeeze... Why would I do...? And I — fainted? Guess I haven't eaten much lately. Never fainted before."

Hit many women before?

He gropes around, notices the bloody makeshift bandage. Pain and memory may be flooding back.

"Where's my shotgun?"

In the well. The river. The compost heap. The poison ivy.

By now I could be up the road, or half-across the river.

"Do keep your arm raised, and press on the wound."

A shape looms in the window. The movement startles him, he gestures with the invisible shotgun, tries to stand.

"Just the cat." I open the kitchen door. Could slip out now but Singa dashes in shaking rain from his mane, meowing his laryngitic meowl. He stretches up, digs considerable claws into my jeans, begging for recognition, affection, food. I disengage him and shake Kibbles into his bowl. Normally shy of strangers,

Singa saunters over to inspect this one on the floor. The lure of blood? The man stares at him, then extends his left hand.

"Did I do that?" He points to the blood and water pooled in the sunken area of the linoleum and pulls himself onto the kitchen chair.

"Never mind," I say. "Nothing can hurt this floor."

"Why don't you tile it?"

Damned impertinent question.

"We bought linoleum on sale last month, but it's too cumbersome to cut and lay myself, and I can't afford..."

Now I've blown it: "I" and "me" instead of "we" and "us." True, Tom dragged in the linoleum but claimed prior appointments in Mauritania, or was it Mauritius, all month.

The tea has cooled. I push his cup closer. He considers the mint floating like seaweed, inhales, sips, then, filtering the leaves with his teeth, downs it. I pour more.

"Does the arm still hurt?"

"I'll live."

"Here's aspirin for the pain, but eat something first. I'll warm the bread, it's fairly fresh. I baked apples from our tree into it."

"You *bake* bread?"

"Fridays, before weekend guests." I spread what's left with butter, also reserved for guests.

In Greek, the word for "guest" and "stranger" are the same: *ksenos*. Do ancient rules of hospitality still...?

The man watches Singa eat. "I had a cat that color once, like coffee that's half milk. Short-haired. Yours must be angora."

"Partially. And only partially mine. He was living wild in the woods and barn. The house stood unoccupied for a year before I — we — moved in. He'd yowl from the magnolia but disappear if anyone looked his way. Last spring we were eating pumpkin pie on the porch when he appeared among the daffodils. I meowed, he turned and trotted across the lawn. I threw my slice and he pounced and consumed it. Probably the milk and eggs he liked, but I planted pumpkins. Anyhow, now he is a real lap cat. Still his own cat, mind you. If I'm away a few days, we leave him food, but when that's gone and no more appears, he loses faith, disappears."

"Got a name?"

"Singa. Lion in — I think it's Malay, or Indonesian."

"Surabaya," he murmurs, studying me.

I turn, sip my cup by the stove. Fragrances of bread, apples, cinnamon warm me despite wet clothes.

Must get him out. "Where do you live?"

"Up the hill and down the road."

"After Mrs. Bryant's, there aren't any houses down the road. It dead-ends in fields."

He keeps glancing out the windows. Suddenly that old cliché about hair standing on end is no more mere cliché. I shiver with a chill not just from wet clothes.

"Is there someone out there?" I ask.

"Imagine they're long gone by now."

"They?" And does he mean, elliptically, *I imagine they're gone,* or the imperative, *You darn well better imagine....*

Beyond the dark magnolia, the sky is darkening fast. The kitchen is dim, I should light...

For the first time I wish for curtains, wish the landlord had cut the corn for a clear field of vision.

It would impede his departure to lock doors now. The minute he leaves, I will.

Futile. Few of the windows close tightly. As the

landlord says, "Anyone who wants can always get in, and you don't want to keep your friends out."

As guests say, better get some decent locks.

The garage better reassemble my car quickly. The hardware store has double bolts, window locks, grills.

Nobody bothers with grills in the country.

I set the warmed bread on a plate before him. One glance at his hands, and I wring out a dishtowel with hot water and pass it over, gingerly. He holds it gingerly, as if unsure what to do with it.

He takes a deep breath.

"I was about to shoot this stag. I'd waited hours. All antlers, he came out of the woods beyond the field. I was ready to fire. Then someone the near side of the field fired at me."

"Why were you about to shoot a stag?"

"Why? F'Chrissakes, it's hunting season!"

"Not on this property. Didn't you see our signs? The landlord won't let anyone hunt on his land. Did you fire?"

His mouth full of bread, he mumbles, avoids my eyes.

"Did either of you hit the deer?"

"Don't think so."

"You know who it was?"

"Didn't waste time looking."

Given the man's unfriendly expression, I cross the living room to the sun porch, closing windows, latching doors, in last spring's exuberance painted red.

"Your bread's good," the man says. "Don't mean to trouble you, but..."

"That's all there was. I thought hunters ate huge breakfasts and carried stacks of sandwiches."

"Guess some do."

"Which one is your house 'down the road'?"

"You sure ask questions."

He finishes his second cup of tea. I forgot the honey

this time. My cheek hurts. I keep my face turned.

"At the moment...until I get settled," he begins, with many pauses, "I'm living down the road...off the road...in the woods...in my car."

"What would you do with a whole dead deer, cook it over the cigarette lighter? The engine?"

He takes another breath. "The people who run the diner where I sometimes eat — it beats MacDonald's — like venison."

Then they should damn well get their own. Not in these woods either. He's probably run up bar bills.

"Where's your family?"

"Family." He seems to be turning over the word. "Family... Pittsburgh... My ex-wife remarried. It's okay." He picks up speed. "She's happy, she kept the house, they were her kids. No sweat leaving Pittsburgh. Too far inland. Lotsa layoffs there. Damned if I'd go on welfare. I paid my debts, filled the car, and left. I'd seen this area in the Navy, and remembered they hire civilians. So I drove here, found the motel, and applied at the base. They said they'd hire me, but there's a freeze on."

"So how are you living?"

"Odd jobs. Enough to wait it out. Trouble is, everyone else needs odd jobs. Locals have first choice. Rightly, of course. But there've been bad feelings around the county."

"Anything to do with whoever shot you?"

He shrugged. "Some guys collect old M1's, AK-47's. Whole damn arsenals."

Great. What next.

I open the fridge. So bare after last weekend, it wobbles. The crabs, quiescent with cold, twitch long stalked eyes and antennae feebly.

"You like crabs?"

"Sure. Scarce in Pennsylvania. I'd considered finding a boat here and setting out trot-lines, but the season's over. The diner serves crab cakes, but at two bucks apiece, so..."

"But the blues are running." I lift the white-speckled black enamel steamer from above the fridge, run an inch of water in the lower compartment, slip the two crabs in the upper, lotta pot for two crabs, and light the flame. Least I can do is feed him before he leaves.

Could all be a cock-and-bull story. Goose-and-deer story. He's just playing for time till he gets his shotgun back, neither of us trusts the other. But what do you do?

"You like them spicy?"

"Sure."

I sprinkle Old Bay Seasoning, drop butter in the silver-dollar-sized pan on the steamer lid. Warming, the crabs scramble against the pot walls. To mask the sounds, which make me think of Dachau, I run water hard on the greens.

Two crabs won't go far, one colander of greens cooks down to one cup.... Can't harvest Jerusalem artichokes till frost, nor is this the moment to dig potatoes. Brown rice takes an hour. Bulgar wheat for tabulleh? He'll think it weird stuff but it's quick.

"Pity the puffballs aren't out yet."

"Some along side the fields."

"Where?" I ask eagerly.

"I'll show you sometime."

Oil into the pan.

Now to tackle an onion, harvested yesterday. I peel the outer skin, translucent and stiff as a beetle's outer wings, down to the inner layers, translucent as — cicada wings. Onion vapors sting my eyes, tears overflow the cut on my cheek. Hurts like hell, and my hands are covered with onion juice. Squinting, I hack blindly, scrape chopped onion into the pan to saute.

At last the crabs stop their desperate skirmish, redden by degrees. I hear the chair scrape, the cup clink, running water.

"I wash up in the state park when the gates aren't locked, or at the diner," he says. "I swam in the Bay the day I arrived but got stung by jellyfish."

"They've disappeared downriver now," I answer through onion tears. "I swam yesterday. Too cold to stay in long."

"I'll clean your table."

"Could you please give me a towel," I call out. "A wet *paper* towel — quickly — "

Above the onion sizzle a paper towel rips.

More water running, then he hands me a damp wad. "Hey, what's the matter?"

"Onions — " The towel hasn't helped. I can't open my eyes.

"You must've scraped your face."

"*You* must've scraped my face."

"When?"

"When you hit me."

"I — I didn't hit — I don't remember hitting you."

"As you came to, after you fainted. Better sit down so you don't faint again."

My eyes hurt, my hurt hurts. Who says redheads are more sensitive to pain than the rest of us?

"Jesus!" He steps closer, takes me by the shoulders. I struggle, push him away but he steers me backwards into the chair, then, ten feet tall, bends down.

"Jeeze, I'm sorry." He daubs my face, then reopens the hydrogen peroxide.

"Damn stuff stings, please don't get it in my eyes."

"Sorry for the trouble, really am."

He pats the abrasion on my cheek, blotting my eyelids with another wet towel. Not liking anyone near my eyes, I veer away. He persists in washing my face, patting it dry. As if I were a child. Then he finds a Band-Aid in the drawer, glues it across my cheek.

"Jeeze, does it hurt?"

"I'll live. How's your arm? You must see a doctor. Wounds fester."

"Later."

Without a steady job, he must lack insurance. I pay my own premiums now, costs a fortune. "Rural hospitals treat uninsured people," I say.

"I'll be okay."

Singa is stalking the steam from the pot. I lower the flame. The onions sauteed, I stir in chicken stock and the bulgar wheat.

"Need some rosemary. You honestly think someone's hanging around outside?"

"Rosemary?"

"For the turnip greens."

"Turnip greens?"

"S'okay, it's still raining. There's basil in the pitcher."

He ties his boot laces, awkwardly, then walks into the dim living room, inspects the porch, looks out windows, doors, starts out the back.

"Wait — " I retrieve his shotgun from the closet. The roll of linoleum falls out and we nearly trip over it. Grabbing the BB gun, I hear the reassuring rattle of BBs in the chamber. I turn off the stove, slip on my slicker, muddy shoes, and run after him.

No cowbell this time.

Chilly. Must be sunset beyond the clouds. Peering through raindrops, we circle the house, the barn, check inside, then head to the sickle of sand by the cove. Rain beats the sand, the tide has erased all footprints: raccoon, gull or human.

"Nice little beach you got." With his good hand he tests the water. "Could still swim."

We pass the old icebox.

"I'll get the Bactine. A beer with the crabs?"

"Would taste good."

I put the Bactine in my pocket, two beers in his, then wonder what the hell I'm doing offering liquor to a could-be alcoholic, rapist, murderer, at the least a bum.

Sudden honking of geese overhead, hundreds, unseen but so low I can hear the brush-beat of their wings. Visitations of strange angels.

Half expecting to hear shots, I say, "He could still be hiding in the cornfield, or the woods."

"They're probably tired of being wet, and gone home."

"They? What are we dealing with, a battalion?"

Whatever answer is lost in the rain. Passing the garden, I snip rosemary, then mint and parsley for the tabbouleh. No healing herbs for wounds.

Leaving shoes and boots by the door, we enter the dark steamy kitchen. I switch on the overhead bulb. Nervous again, he checks every window.

"Yes," I say, "we'd be great targets, shooting gallery ducks."

"Certain things you live with."

"Thanks."

"Sorry."

He props his shotgun by the stove. I lean the BB gun beside it, start the turnip greens. Generally I eat on the sun porch, but even with windows closed it's cold these evenings, and if anyone's out there...

The man disappeares into the downstairs lavatory. I head upstairs. Rain drips into the roasting pan in the bedroom. Dry jeans, sweater, socks. I comb my snarls, peek under the Band-Aid, examine my cheek. I'll live.

Could he fit in Niko's old sweatshirt?

Downstairs, he's opening pot lids. The bulgar

swells to fill the pan, the turnip greens cook down, the crabs are coral. Singa is crazy with the smell. I'm starved. And he must be. Literally.

He washes the table, shoves it near the window seat. I set out crabs, mallets, greens, bulgar, melted butter, bowls for rinsing fingers, a bucket for crab shells. Singa paws the table's edge.

The man sits against the wall between the windows. His good hand probes a crab, the other is useless.

"Don't muck up that fancy bandage."

I pull my chair closer, hammer and pry the shells, extracting the fragile meat, which ultimately doesn't amount to much. I fill the backs with gills and entrails for Singa who licks them clean, then stretches up to dig his claws into the man's thigh.

"Ill-mannered stray," I apologize. "I'll put him outside."

"He's okay here. I guess you'd probably call me a — a temporary stray." The man sucks the crab's slender walking legs.

"Maybe you're starting a new phase of life. Here, try this tabbouleh — bulgar wheat — like rice, only better."

"I ate stuff like this in the Middle East. With the Navy."

He lapses into silence while he eats most of both crabs and the tabbouleh, starts the second beer, excuses himself to the lavatory. I eat the turnip greens, cold now.

He settles back on the window seat. "Been here long?" As if he guesses I haven't.

"We rented the farm 'as is' last March. So much work still. Roof leaks, you see this floor, the landlord won't repair — he plans to tear the house down anyway. I can fix whatever I can't live with, or whatever I can fix. At least living here costs half what it does in town, and God, I love this place, wish he'd sell it to me, wish I could afford — Sorry. I'm chattering nonstop like my grandmother in her final years of solitude."

Back and forth between "I" and royal, phantom "we" again. The "we" is partly true: friends helped move and plant and paint. But essentially, and in essence for the first time in my life, the full responsibility is mine. Sometimes: too full.

Rain heavier. When and how will this guy get on his way homeward. Carward. Don't even know his name. Nor he mine. As if by mutual agreement. He sits watching the rain against the window.

"Some day we'd like to raise two or three dairy cows," I say, to break the silence, although this is the first time such an idea has come into my head. I certainly don't want to be tied down to livestock, milking schedules. "Well, heifers, if anything."

"Holsteins," he says. "Best butterfat content."

And suddenly the wet meadows of my mind blossom with fat black-and-white calves, like litters of overgrown and ungainly Dalmatians.

"Can you support yourself farming?" he asks.

"We'd like to be self-sufficient in food."

"But for rent?" he persists.

"People send me articles to translate. From Greek. Modern. Mostly business. I'd prefer archaeology, architecture, literature, but no, you can't support a farm on that."

"You Greek?"

"No, just that my father taught physics in Athens. I married a Greek."

I don't mention how impetuously, romantically, briefly. Nor how ultimately boring a later, well-thought-out, marriage. Nor what, or who, happened in between, or since. Perhaps this time I've married a farm. This merely rented farm.

"Our ship docked overnight in Piraeus." His voice sounds increasingly weary. "I walked around the port."

"I used to do that, after school, imagining centuries of boats sunk into layers of muck on that harbor floor."

"Could find old boats out there." His good arm gestures toward the river. "Indian dug-outs. Fishing boats. Pirates. British and American warships. Interesting, that museum near the base."

Bet he also goes there to wash. "I send guests there to sightsee."

How I welcome guests on Friday evenings or Saturdays. I'm both relieved and sorry when Sunday night they depart, often reiterating their concern about my staying alone all week. Now winter's coming, few guests will.

As for this — guest — *ksenos:* eyes heavy, he's finished the beer, is winding down rapidly. I don't know what to do. When a cat is undecided, he washes himself. I rinse our dishes in the sink. Let the pots soak. I'll scrub when he leaves.

"Some fruit?" How pocked and green the apples, how few grapes left. Their thick dusty-blue skin is sweet, the lucid fruit inside tart. I swallow seeds too. Maybe, as Grandmother predicted, a Concord grapevine will grow inside me. "Real Concords, try them. I love Concords but the season's over already."

He eats two grapes, slouches back.

I heat the last inch of milk in the fridge with some honey. Grandmother always drank some at bedtime. I set the cup on the table. He drinks it slowly, settles back, slumps, head tilted against the wall, eyes slits.

I don't feel like heading to the beach alone tonight.

"Shall we go dump crab shells in the river to feed the fish? Then I'll give you my flashlight to see your way home."

No response.

I relent, put the bucket of crabshells out under the magnolia. Raining harder anyway. Between Singa and the raccoons, the yard will be a mess tomorrow but think of their pleasure.

The man lies sprawled on the window seat, sweat-shirt pillowing his head, asleep, or passed out. Leaving the flashlight beside him, I take the blanket from the sofa, where I slept last night to avoid the upstairs leaks, and spread it over him. He doesn't budge. I cover the silver fruit bowl to keep out bugs, switch off the kitchen light, leave one shining through from the living room, retreat upstairs with the BB gun.

Rain drips into the roasting pan in my bedroom. From my bed I normally see the pale outline of the beach and shimmer of waves even by starlight. Can't see anywhere tonight. I have to believe no one is outside.

Definitely someone inside. He snores. Will I also hear him wake up? What's my alternative? Pry the creaky trap door and hide in the cellar? Crouch on those stairs going nowhere?

I close my bedroom door quietly. No lock or hook. Better stay dressed. Propping pillows on the bed, I lean back in the dark, one hand on the BB gun. Should've taken his shotgun too. Still could.

He might wake, then, or later, come searching. I'd at least be able to defend myself. I'll tiptoe down, take the flashlight, walk up the road, call from — wake up — deaf Mrs. Bryant's?

Tom's right: a woman out here alone...

Rain pummels the roof. Even when it lessens, the ceiling continues its drip-drip-drip into the pan, unmufflled by a towel.

I forgot to wash the dishes.

Tomorrow I'll get him to a doctor.

Tomorrow he'll be gone. Along with silver pitcher and bowls, stereo, computer.

All in one hand?

Must fight sleep.

The rain stops. The full moon slips as if blown through the clouds, turns the dark waves platinum.

Fatigue overwhelms.

Black-and-white cattle stampede through my dreams, shelter under the big magnolia.

I wake late. The sun streams through the window. Gypsy Summer. No sound from below. I shower, put on fresh clothes.

The kitchen is empty. The blanket and sweatshirt lie folded on the window seat. Dishes drain in the rack. Even the crab steamer. The floor is washed. Nothing seems missing but the flowered towel; trust he's thrown that away. The bucket is on the porch, clean, no mess of crabshells around. Except for the cut on my cheek, it's as if nothing had happened.

Almost warm on the beach. Reddened crabs float by. The ghost of a boot print among eel grass, bare footprints at the edge of the wavelets. Did he swim? I hope the wound stayed dry.

Geese overfly as I head toward the house. The lavender towel drips on the clothesline; I don't inspect it closely. Even were the dress hanging here, I'd never —

The phone!

"The part for your transmission came," Joe says. "I'm short-handed — hunting season, you know — but I can deliver your car around six. Could you drive me back?"

"Gladly."

Beside the phone is a note: *Sorry for — everything* is crossed out. Then: *Sorry for the trouble. Thanks for everything. Yours tr —* The "*s*" and "*tr*" are scratched out. The note is signed: *Your other stray. P.S. I borrowed an apple.*

Those sad apples.

Of course I make inquiries. The hospital needs a name in order to raise anything in their computer. Nobody recalls a gun wound lately.

"This isn't the inner city," says the duty nurse over the phone, "though every fall some fool hunter will spray himself or someone else with buckshot."

Driving Joe home, I ask about strangers around, hunters.

"Got me a doe last week," he says. "I'll bring you some venison."

"Thanks, I'm okay, but if you catch any extra bluefish..."

I drop by four diners along the main highway, order a Diet Pepsi at each. No one remembers a stubbled, redheaded man. No vehicles with Pennsylvania plates.

At the top of the hill, I bang on Mrs. Bryant's door. "Have you noticed any strangers around? Were you disturbed by all the shooting yesterday? "

"Oh, you want to order an afghan, dear? And my boys filtered more honey."

I buy a quart jar of honey, once was a mayonnaise jar then probably held oysters. And I drive down to where her road ends. The field is empty, the woods show barely a rabbit track through the blackberry briars.

I call the landlord. "I'm afraid people were hunting on your land."

"What can you do, hunters will hunt. If they bother you, call the sheriff."

Late in the night, buoyed by the Pepsis, I finish the translations. Intricate, lucrative, dull. I call Baltimore. Friends invite me to stay with them. Lunches and dinners are scheduled, a concert with Tom, who wants me to come for longer: why don't

I move back to town for the winter?

After last night's incident, that suggestion is tempting. Perhaps I should reconsider. Just come down here weekends with friends. And what about snow storms, they don't come often, but when they do, who'd plough this dirt road?

I leave Kibbles and water under the overhang of the back door, enough to last two days. If mice, squirrels, raccoons, rabbits, birds, pilfer more than their share, Singa will disappear in disgust at human perfidy, and catch his own dinner.

I bag apples and turnip greens for whomever in town might cook them. Locking the doors, I hide the key in its crevice. Must remember locks at the hardware store.

Four days later, I leave town with regret, relief, a briefcase of new work including an avant-garde Greek novel to translate, four grocery sacks, curled hair, a mild hangover, a new blue silk dress I may never wear again. I won't return to town for a month or six.

Forgot to buy locks. At the mailbox where the dirt road begins, I pause for accumulated bills, and the view: long beige fields of corn, greengold fields of soy beans, brown fields stubbled with hacked-off tobacco stalks, fields outlined by hedgerows turning scarlet and gold, punctuated by single dark green cypresses.

Suddenly three deer bound across the road. How beautiful October is here! And November should also be. Swans due mid-November. During the rare blizzards in December, January or February, I'll learn cross-country skiing. Turnips, kale, broccoli will poke green through the snow, potatoes and Jerusalem artichokes wait underneath. And I'll consider a couple of hens, a rooster even.

I will be all right here.

Singa stretches on the back step. Despite my

longer absence, he has enough food, the water bowl is full. He follows me inside.

God, what? The floor gleams — blue — the new linoleum! The landlord changed his mind, took pity on this place, renovated —

Then I notice near the silver bowl a beer carton overflowing with Concord grapes, and in the middle, one Red Delicious.

BENEDICTUS ES DOMINE

Thank You that I'm curled up here with a lover, this lover, my lover, not mine, but with me ten years (albeit for one he strayed).

Thank You that I finally strayed as well, with equal success and anguish.

Thank You that before our loving this morning, he cleaned up the kitchen after the resident mice. Thank You for returning the orange tom from across the soy bean field so he'll tackle our mice again, and that he merely scares them back into their walls, retreat forestalling slaughter.

Thank You for swans in the cove, deer in the wood, geese overhead, and No Hunting at least on Sunday.

Thank You for propelling my daughter this way with her loaves of cinnamon bread, also that this particular morning she hasn't knocked yet. Thank You that she got through medical school and without my selling the house, and that both miraculous sons have survived their youth.

Thank You for the Hispanic lady with pancake make-up and platinum eye-shadow, escaped from several Latin dictators, and that she xeroxed our 876-page manuscript for just four cents per page and claimed she adored what she read between feeds.

Thank You that despite Your frequent absence from the macrocosm beyond, You still hover, if never enough.

Thank You for Your patience even with those of us who reject You on intellectual principle.

Thank You for letting me now again lay me down to sleep after such loving. And in fact, should You choose that I die before I awake, You'd be getting a bargain in gratitude, whereas if You wait till I'm ailing, old, alone and quite likely daft, You'll hear symphonies of complaints.

So take what You can while I'm worth the take. And thank You for waiting this long.

ROOT SOUP, EASTER MONDAY

The soup cries out for roots: turnips, parsnips, even a clumsy rutabaga —

Again we test the scumming broth of Easter's turkey bones in my copper cauldron.

But this is spring. Saturday I cleared out stones, planted seeds, cubed potatoes rife with sprouts, buried them in one last row. Then the news came: my father just died.

Tonight I mince last winter's parsley with garlic, onions, cabbage, bay leaves from a Christmas wreath.

My father often told me how a soldier, young and hungry, asked shelter from a peasant babushka. "I have no food," she said. Then from his knapsack he took a pebble and dropped it in her kettle.

Soon their soup was bubbling with unearthed miracles of vegetables, and they ate all week.

Tonight Ann offers carrots, David two potatoes, Sergei beets to make it borscht. I throw in sausage, peppers, thyme.

"Each guest is sent to us by God" — an old Caucasian song my father sang.

Now the soup pot simmers high as it simmered in his house, overflows into our bowls.

He must have left a stone to me.

* * *

My father was given an extraordinary service at Arlington Cemetery: honor guard of one hundred men, rifle volleys, six white horses pulling the caisson, one black horse with stirrups reversed. Two weeks later came the memorial service at the Russian church, with two bassos in the a cappella choir up in the loft over our heads.

Each service, attended by different friends, was followed by a sort of wake at my house. I laid out a cauldron of "stone soup," his favorite caviar, herring with sour cream, curried lentils, sausages, salads, cheeses, wine and vodka, three kinds of cakes baked by neighbors.

I could not find an eel.

CODICIL

About burning, I've changed my mind.

Today, in a mulberried graveyard above the Chesapeake Bay, dogwood in bloom, sails on the waves, I sit on the brick base of a tomb and write. On top of bones. Like an off-duty harpooner engraving the ribs of a whale.

One marble rectangle covers two tenants: a man, *born 1884, in Knoxville, Tennessee, died 1956;* his wife, *born 1889, in Austin, Nevada, died 1976.*

Do they lie side by side or, twenty years between deaths, would she rest on top?

I too was born inland, Missouri, a Midwesterner with uncurbed lust for the sea, also fled to the coast.

I've not returned to my father's plot in Arlington to inspect that stiff upright stone. As if his packet of cinders and ash required so much weight. To save space on our shrunken planet my stepmother talked him into cremation.

A sensible choice for all, I'd agreed.

But now I've resolved: Plant me whole, here, on this bluff. Watched over by herons and gulls and swans, I'll dissolve on my own like jellyfish in the sun.

With luck, I'll lie with a lover. Passers by en route to the beach who shortcut through these graves overgrown with rain-soaked clover might find our granite slab wide enough to stretch out on. Let them write, scrimshaw, make love over our bones.

My gregarious father, who lay with many women and also loved oceans, would have liked that.

Also available from Signal Books
in the
TIDEWATER FICTION SERIES

Everything Thats All
1931-1942

by Shirley Graves Cochrane

163pp. Hardcover. Fiction. 14 original illustrations LC 91-10617 CIP (ISBN 0930095-07-3) $16.50. "An important contribution to our literature." *William Friday, President Emeritus, University. of North Carolina.*

And related works by Tidewater Series authors

Elisavietta Ritchie

Tightening the Circle over Eel Country
Poems. Paper. 110pp. ISBN 87491-300-x $4.75

Raking the Snow
Poems. Paper. 55pp. ISBN 0-931846-21-8 $4.00

The Dolphin's Arc : Poems on Endangered Creatures of the Sea ed. Ritchie
Anthology of poems by 109 distinguished poets. Paper. 165pp. ISBN 0-930526-11-2 $10.95

Shirley Graves Cochrane

Family and Other Strangers
Poems. Paper. 57pp. ISBN 86-050-180-x $7.00

Shirley Graves and Betsy Bowman

The Jones Family
Reproduction of 1937 manuscript of children's saga of imagined ideal family. Facsimile portions of original manuscript and illustrations introduce each chapter.
Paper. 45pp. ISBN 0-9609062-2-3 $10.00

Maxine Combs

Swiming out of the Collective Unconscious
Poems. Paper. 35pp. ISBN 0-9612158-3-6 $3.00

Elisabeth Stevens

HORSE and CART Stories from the Country
Paper. 104 pp. ISBN0-9612158-52 $7.95

Folk Art and Literature from Signal

El Kanil Man of Lightning
A legend of Jacaltenango, Guatemala
recorded and written by Victor Montejo.
English version by Wallace Kaufman
ISBN 0-930095-01-4 Poetry. Paper 63pp. $6.00

Hans Anderson: His Life and Work
Catalogue of Leelanau Co. Michigan Historical Society exibition of Scandinavian folk painter and sculptor. Paper. 76pp 147 illustrations in color and half-tone.
ISBN 0-930095-10-3 $19.00

Place orders to: **Signal Books**
P.O. Box 940
Carrboro, NC 27510
Phone (919) 929-5985
Fax (919) 929-5986

About Signal Books

Signal Books is a small but growing independent publishing house operating from a train car and an antique bookmobile in Carrboro, NC.

Founded in 1985 by a former professor of modern British literature at the University of North Carolina at Chapel Hill, Signal began by publishing adult nonfiction, concentrating on the U.S. Constitution and constitutional issues.

It has since expanded to include among its titles works as varied as the catalogue of a Scandinavian-American folk artist, a consumer-oriented insider's guide to investing, and a historical reference work on Nicaragua.

Flying Time is the second work in Signal's new focus on serious literary fiction and personal narrative. We are committed to working closely with our authors to produce works of lasting value in a form and graphic design worthy of the quality of the text.

We try actively to be environmentally and socially responsible — printing only on recycled paper with soybean ink; providing copies of any of our titles free to adult literacy education groups; and encouraging free use of our texts for braille, large type, audio-taped and other special editions for the handicapped.

About this book

Flying Time was laid out and composed on a 486 IBM clone using Microsoft Windows and Aldus PageMaker PM4. It was set at 1000 d.p.i on a LaserMaster True Tech 1000 printer in Postscript Palatino. It was printed on 55 pound Huron natural acid-free recycled paper in Smythe sewn signatures using soybean ink by Thomson-Shore of Dexter, Michigan. Cover design and illustrations were by Michael Brown. Four color separation for the cover was made by Image Arts of Lansing, Michigan.

For free rights to use any portion of this text for versions for the handicapped, write to Signal Books Box 940 Carrboro, NC 27510.

Elisavietta Ritchie is a widely published and highly praised poet, short story writer, journalist, translator, and photographer. Her many contributions to dozens of the best periodicals and anthologies in America have frequently been prize winners.

Her *Tightening the Circle over Eel Country* won the Great Lakes College Association New Writers' Award for the best first book of poetry in 1975-76. She has received four PEN Syndicated Fiction awards, two Poetry Society of America annual awards, four Individual Artist Grants from the District of Columbia Commission on the Arts, and several fellowships from the Virginia Center for the Creative Arts.

Her readings at The Library of Congress, the Folger Library, at numerous conferences, and on numerous campuses have met with enthusiastic response and she was selected as visiting poet for the United States Information Agency in the Far East, the Balkans, and Brazil.

She is founder of Wineberry Press and former president of Washington Writer's Publishing House.

Flying Time is the first full-length collection of Ritchie's prose. It ranges from memoirs of visits to her Russian relatives to stories and a novella of imperiled rural solitude in the Chesapeake Bay area.

The pain and obligation of love —difficult choices, jealousy, even hate — as well as the passion and fulfillment of love are explored in these tightly written fictions. In them Ritchie shows that caring — for parents, lovers, children, friends, old people, animals — is never entirely satisfactory, never easy.

All of the writing is permeated with Ritchie's personal vitality and her intense, sophisticated involvement with nature. She excels in vibrant description, a poet's command of language, and the powerful concentration of the sometimes poignant, sometimes humorous, often biting "half-stories."